EVERLASTING LOVE DANCE HALL DAYS DISCOTHEQUE NIGHTS

GERRY CULLEN

Copyright © 2024 GERRY CULLEN

All rights reserved

The characters and events portrayed in this book are fictitious. Any similarity to real persons, living or dead, is coincidental and not intended by the author.

No part of this book may be reproduced, or stored in a retrieval system, or transmitted in any form or by any means, electronic, mechanical, photocopying, recording, or otherwise, without express written permission of the publisher.

ISBN-13: 9798343146622
ISBN-10: 1477123456

Cover design by: Art Painter
Library of Congress Control Number: 2018675309
Printed in the United States of America

THIS BOOK IS DEDICATED TO MY MUM AND DAD

CONTENTS

Title Page
Copyright
Dedication
ALSO BY GERRY CULLEN
ABOUT THE AUTHOR GERRY CULLEN
EVERLASTING LOVE

EVERLASTING LOVE	1
EVERLASTING LOVE	5
SWINGING SIXTIES SATURDAY DANCE	10
SUMMERTIME CITY '75	24
LOVE CHEAT	36
BOBBY AND JACKIE'S STORY	47
PARTY NIGHT	57
NEW YEAR'S EVE BALL	69
THE HOLE IN THE WALL	80
THE LEGEND BEGINS	81
TEENAGERS IN THE SWINGING SIXTIES	90

THAT'S ONE SMALL STEP FOR MAN, ONE GIANT LEAP FOR ME!	102
SOUL FINGER	111
GIMME ... GIMME ... GOOD LOVIN'	120
SWEET SOUL MUSIC	129
LOVE, MUSIC AND DANCING	138
SAM AND MARTIN'S STORY	139
THE WALL FLOWER STORY	151
BALI HAI	162
NEW VENTURE SINGLES	172
CHRISTMAS AND NEW YEAR	183
LOVE AND MEMORIES ... A COMPANY DANCE STORY	195
DISCOTHEQUE	207
AM I IN LOVE ... OR WHAT?	208
MAN ABOUT TOWN	218
IT MECCA ME SICK!	224
BRINGING ON THE GOOD TIMES	232
ZODIAC/MIRAGE	239
THE EVENT 2025 ... REUNION	251
THE VATICAN MONSIGNOR	263
SKY HIGH!	267
EVERLASTING LOVE	269
MY NEXT PRESENTATION	271
	278

About The Author	279
Praise For Author	281
Books By This Author	285

ALSO BY GERRY CULLEN

BETWEEN WORLDS: MY TRUE COMA STORY

SKY HIGH: COTE D'AZUR

ANGEL'S EYES:

CHRISTMAS ANGELS

THE VATICAN MONSIGNOR

THE SAVIOUR'S COMING

IT'S A KIND OF LOVE

DCS MACCORMAC OXFORD

SANCTUM SANCTORUM

EVERLASTING LOVE

DANCE HALL DAYS

DISCOTHEQUE NIGHTS

ABOUT THE AUTHOR
GERRY CULLEN

My first book, BETWEEN WORLDS: MY TRUE COMA STORY, is a true adaptation of what happened to me, before and after, having major open heart surgery at Leeds General Infirmary in March 2018.

It is a very real and true account of the "gift" I received after being in an induced coma.

All of my books to date, SKY HIGH! COTE D'AZUR, ANGEL'S EYES/CHRISTMAS ANGELS, THE VATICAN MONSIGNOR, and IT'S A KIND OF LOVE are adapted from my series of stories, written for television.
I had never written books or for television prior to being in a coma.

My very real and true story continues today!

FOLLOW MY STORY ON TWITTER - @GerryCullen15

EVERLASTING LOVE

DANCE HALL DAYS

DISCOTHEQUE NIGHTS

They say if you can remember the Sixties, you weren't there!

Well, I can categorically say that I do remember the Sixties and the Seventies, and I was there!

That is what this book is all about ... do you remember?

We were all young, innocent, and inexperienced back then!

All you needed was a place to go, sensational music, way out fashions, fabulous memorable days ... and luck to just maybe fall for a girl and vice versa ... we were all young teenagers in those days.

This book is a journey down memory lane, back to a time when everything was different in so many ways.

I hope you enjoy all the stories featured in this nostalgic trip back in time when we were all growing up together in the Swinging Sixties and the sensational Seventies!

EVERLASTING LOVE

WONDERFUL MEMORIES OF

BRADFORD MECCA

Do you have fond memories of the Mecca Locarno on Manningham Lane in the Sixties and Seventies?

Were you a regular dancer at the famous ballroom?

The Bradford Mecca was the place to be, and the place to be seen in those days.

For me it was the start of everything!

While at College my friends and I decided to visit the famous Hole in the Wall near Sunwin House and then the Mecca on Friday and Saturday nights.

We had some memorable nights out at both venues. Girls would dance round their handbags to Tamla Motown and Soul music, and we would dance close but just admire them.

We were too shy to talk to girls in those days!

Girls wore their miniskirts or psychedelic mini dresses, and we wore twenty-four-inch bell bottoms with coloured shirts that had poke your eyes out collars and kipper ties ... boy did we look the bee's knees!

We certainly dressed to impress in the Sixties and Seventies!

We were all young, innocent, and inexperienced back then!

All you needed was a place to go, sensational music, way out fashions, fabulous memorable days ... and luck to just maybe fall for a girl and vice versa.

We were all young teenagers in those days.

The Mecca had a DJ with a records section playing Sixties hits and the Bobby Brook Band played "live" music. The revolving stage changeover was to an instrumental called Time is Tight.

Bradford Mecca Locarno had a canopy above its iconic entrance. It also boasted infrared heaters above the frontage for patrons queuing outside on chilly winter evenings.

Inside the venue was a large modern ballroom. It also had air vents which produced cool temperatures discreetly placed around the edge of the dance floor.

On entry into the music complex ladies and gentlemen were met by the elegantly named "Ladies Boudour" and the "Stag Room" which offered the latest in luxury. There were mirrors everywhere in both rooms, and a cloak room which was overseen by one of the Mecca staff.

The first floor or balcony overlooked the huge dance floor, and it boasted dimly lit tables with red light shades and flock wallpaper on both floors.

It also had an area where refreshments could be purchased mostly chips and burgers, coffee and cola.

We took full advantage of this once inside the huge venue.

I remember a blind date meet up in the late Sixties with someone inside the Ballroom. I was only 14 at the time and it felt daring. Things did not work out, but I have never forgotten about that now laughable situation! I was really embarrassed about the whole thing!

Now, over 50 years later I have decided to write about the Bradford Mecca story in this book along with other stories about similar venues in the area.

I call it fiction based on fact!

All my stories are comedy/drama based so expect some laughs along the way!

If you read the stories about the Mecca, you may just find me there!

We all have lots of memories of the Mecca, and I think you will find this book heartwarming, entertaining and interesting.

It certainly is a trip down memory lane for all of us.

How would I describe it?

I can relate to all the stories, and I think you will too!

The Bradford Mecca Locarno was not just an iconic venue it was a place where lots of us met for the first time ... where memories were made at a time when everything was just beginning to happen in all our lives.

Of course, none of this would have happened had I not acquired my "Gift" for writing out of my induced coma at Leeds General Infirmary in March 2018.

That is another story!

Now, six and a half years later ...

I have written 122 Television series and published 6 books to date all out of my coma!

Royalties from all my books will eventually be sent to Cardiac Care at Leeds General Infirmary.

My very real and true story continues today!

Follow me on TWITTER/X @GerryCullen15

FACEBOOK - GERRY Cullen (Author page)

EVERLASTING LOVE

It's back to the Sixties and Seventies for this pop music/dancing themed comedy/drama set of stories.

Bradford Mecca Locarno is the iconic venue, and the place to be where boy meets girl in a relaxed atmosphere set against the backdrop of the music of the era!

Six stories of looking and finding love, dancing, taking chances and meeting "the one" or dreaming about that one special person.

Atmospheric and exhilarating this was an innocent time and shows how life used to be in that golden era.

The Internet, laptops, tablets, and mobile phones had not yet been invented and were way into the future!

All you needed back then was a place to go, sensational music, way out fashions to wear, fabulous memorable days ... and luck to just maybe fall for a girl and vice versa. It was all very innocent.

Sex was never on anyone's minds!

Back then you would make each other's night with a kiss or peck on the cheek.

Several other stories feature in my book, and they are also bound to bring back lots of wonderful memories never to be forgotten!

This is how it used to be in the Sixties and Seventies!

EVERLASTING LOVE
DANCE HALL DAYS
DISCOTHEQUE NIGHTS

EVERLASTING LOVE	
SWINGING SIXTIES SATURDAY DANCE	12
SUMMERTIME CITY '75	23
LOVE CHEAT	33
BOBBY AND JACKIE'S STORY	43
PARTY NIGHT	51
NEW YEAR'S EVE BALL	60

THE HOLE IN THE WALL	
THE LEGEND BEGINS	69
TEENAGERS IN THE SWINGING SIXTIES	77
THAT'S ONE SMALL STEP FOR MAN, ONE GIANT LEAP FOR ME	86
SOUL FINGER	94
GIMME ... GIMME ... GOOD LOVIN'	102
SWEET SOUL MUSIC	110
LOVE, MUSIC AND DANCING	
SAM AND MARTIN'S STORY	117
THE WALLFLOWER STORY	128
BALI HAI	137

NEW VENTURE SINGLES	146
CHRISTMAS AND NEW YEAR	155
LOVE AND MEMORIES ... A COMPANY DANCE STORY	165
DISCOTHEQUE	
AM I IN LOVE ... OR WHAT?	175
MAN ABOUT TOWN	184
IT MECCA ME SICK!	189
BRINGING ON THE GOOD TIMES	195
ZODIAC/MIRAGE	201
THE EVENT 2025 ... REUNION	225

SWINGING SIXTIES SATURDAY DANCE

June 1968 ... early Saturday evening, the Mecca Locarno, Manningham Lane, Bradford.

The new venue has a canopy above its iconic entrance. It also boasts infrared heaters above the frontage for patrons queuing outside on chilly winter evenings.

Inside the venue is a large modern ballroom. It also has air vents which produce cool temperatures discreetly placed around the edge of the dance floor.

On entry into the music complex ladies and gentlemen are met by the elegantly named "Ladies Boudour" and the "Stag Room" which offer the latest in luxury. There are mirrors everywhere in both rooms, and a cloak room which is overseen by one of the Mecca staff.

The first floor or balcony overlooks the huge dance

floor, and it boasts dimly lit tables with red light shades. It also has an area where refreshments can be purchased.

You can walk round the entire ballroom from one end to the other. In the lower part of the venue there is a large bar boasting everything you could want drink wise. There is also a smaller discreet and secluded venue called "Bali Hai" for those who want a more intimate evening.

Above the dance floor are 35,000 Italian made light bulbs which when lit give the impression of a starlit sky at night.

Manager, Keith Forbes is in talks with his staff in his office ...

Mike, Pete, Derek, and Frank are the burly "doormen" in charge of who gets in to the prestigious venue ...

In walks resident Band Leader, Bobby Brook ...

Bobby is in his mid-forties, has jet black hair, five foot ten, brown eyes and possesses a positive approach to life!

"Sorry, fellas" greets Bobby (Smiling)

"I didn't know it was meeting time" adds Bobby (Looks sincere)

"It's OK, Bob ... come on in, your invited to our little get together" replies Keith (Smiling)

Keith is in his late forties, has a bald head, blue eyes and looks dramatic in his black and white combo ...

"Well, OK then, but not for long ... we're undertaking rehearsals" adds Bobby (Looks serious)

Bobby is the Leader of the resident Bobby Brook Band, and they provide the "live" music in between change over from the records section.

Resident DJ, Martin Twist (Not real name) is a well-respected music man who recently worked at the Spinning Disc in Leeds city Centre.

"So, what's on the agenda, Keith?" asks Bobby (Looks concerned)

"Well, we're putting together a new disco session on Wednesday evenings for the teenagers ... and there will be a licensed disco for the over 18s in the Bali Hai room" replies Keith (Looks pleased)

"What about us?" asks doorman Mike (Looks puzzled)

"We had a few complaints last week, Mike" replies Keith (Looks serious)

"Complaints ... what about?" asks Derek (Looks also puzzled)

"A little over handled handling" explains Keith (Looks concerned)

"Can you recall the incident?" asks Keith

"To be honest, Keith ... we've had a few lately" explains Frank (Looks serious)

"Let's just try and take the heat out of the situation fellas" asks Keith (Looks concerned)

"In what way, Keith?" asks Derek (Looks concerned)

"Don't be too strict about dress code" advises Keith

"If someone genuinely forgets their tie, let them in" adds Keith

"Gently remind them to wear it next time" instructs Keith (Looks serious)

"We don't really have any problems with the ladies" advises Keith (Sounds relieved)

"Gentle persuasion?" asks Mike (Looks stunned)

"Yes, that's it you've hit the nail on the head" adds Keith

"If for instance if someone comes without a jacket but is wearing something similar, let them in" explains Keith (Smiles)

"The friendly approach?" replies Bobby (Looks serious)

"Yes, we don't want to turn customers away do we, they are our lifeline" explains Keith (Looks stern)

"OK, we understand, Keith" replies Frank (Looks serious)

"Firm but friendly" adds Derek (Looks sincere)

"Exactly" adds Keith (Smiling)

Keith turns to Bobby Brook ...

"Bobby we're trying out a new change over theme from the DJ to the live Band section and vice versa" advises Keith (Smiles)

"What have you got in mind, Keith?" asks Bobby

(Looks serious)

"I was hoping that you might have a few ideas, Bob" replies Keith (Smiles)

"Well, as a matter of fact, I have been working on one or two" advises Bobby (Smiling)

"What kind of ideas?" adds Keith (Smiles)

"Maybe a Soul instrumental for the changeover" replies Bobby

"Yes, OK ... we can try it tonight if you're ready" advises Keith (Smiling)

"Has the new DJ, Martin Twist arrived?" asks Bobby

"He's just entering the building" advises Keith (Looks out of window)

"Well, we will run through the changeover sequence to see if it works" explains Bobby (Looks serious)

Martin Twist knocks on Keith's door and enters the meeting ...

Bobby and Martin co-operate and settle on a recent familiar Soul instrumental and decide to try it out.

Meanwhile, Keith greets the door staff and checks out the new facilities.

STAGS FOR MEN ... HENS FOR WOMEN

The elegantly named Ladies Boudoir has 45 full length mirrors and plush decor.

In the Stag room there is also a certain type of luxury. It is also fitted out with 45 more mirrors and there are cloak rooms in both facilities. Luxury with a capital "L"

Bradford Mecca Locarno is advertised as entertainment for all ages.

It holds special dance themed nights throughout the week.

It really is the place to be in the Swinging Sixties and it is extremely popular with night time revelers!

Mark and Ray are young teenagers, and they are planning their first visit to the Locarno.

Mark is 17 and Ray is 19. They both attend the same College in Bradford.

Mark is six feet tall, has blue eyes, brown hair, and of average good looks,

Ray is five foot 10, has green eyes, brown hair, and wears spectacles.

He is also of average good looks.

Mark and Ray decided to meet outside the Bradford Library Theatre in the City Centre at 7pm ...

They are both excited to be going to the new Locarno venue ...

"Hi, Mark" shouts Ray (Smiling)

"You look very mod" adds Ray

"So do you" replies Mark (Smiles)

"Well, it's finally arrived ... our big night out" advises Ray (Looks excited)

"Yes, at last" adds Mark (Looks equally excited)

They both begin to picture the night ahead and what it might hold for them ...

"We've no need to rush" advises Ray (Smiles)

Mark and Ray make their way on foot to Manningham Lane. No cars back then both were at college. It was all done by bus or train and arrangements were made by word of mouth, letter, or telephone call.

It was a free environment. There was no Internet or such electronic gadgets back then. Yet everything ran smoothly, and it was a very modern place to be and to grow up in.

Mark and Ray eventually reach the very brightly lit Mecca Locarno and are greeted by the door staff ...

The door men are all wearing black dinner suits with a white shirt and bow tie ...

"Your both early tonight" greets Frank (Smiles)

"Yes, it's our first time" replies Ray (Looks excited)

"Well, you're both very welcome ... I am Keith, General Manager of the venue" greets Keith (Smiling)

"Glad to see your both suited and booted" adds Keith

"Nice ties, lads" advises Derek (Smiling)

"This way for entry into the Ballroom" explains Keith (Points the way)

Mark and Ray pay the admittance fee to enter the Ballroom ...

The lady behind the Kiosk is called Barbara (also new to the Mecca)

"Have a nice evening" adds Barbara (Smiling)

"Thank you" replies Ray (Looks excited)

"This way lads" advises Keith (Points the way forward)

Mark and Ray enter the luxurious gentlemen's STAG ROOM.

It has a wall full of mirrors, a cloakroom with an attendant, where you could have your shoes shined free of charge and free hair cream!

"Now this is what I call luxury" advises Mark (Smiling)

"Yes, this certainly is the place to be" quips Ray (Looks excited)

"I can see us becoming part of the furniture here" replies Mark (Looks happy)

"What do you mean?" asks Ray (Looks bewildered)

"It's just an omen, Ray ... a feeling" adds Mark (Sounds excited)

Mark and Ray step out of the Stag Room into the extra-large Ballroom.

It is distinctly opulent in reds, flocked wallpaper and dimly lit red shaded lamps are on all the tables and walls of the Ballroom.

It has an upper balcony and there are two bars on the

lower level. One of the bars is behind the revolving stage and another at the rear of the dance floor. There are tables and chairs on both floors and a fast-food diner selling chips with everything on the balcony as you enter the main concourse.

Above the ceiling there is a multi-light star system and various coloured balloons in a caged basket above the dance floor. There is a large clock to the rear of the dance floor ... this is so you can keep an eye on the time for the last bus home!

Live music is currently playing by the impressive Bobby Brook Band which has three singers, comprising of two females and a male. They are playing popular "live" renditions of Sixties pop music and are very good at what they do!

The Band suddenly starts to play the changeover theme ... Time Is Tight ... at which the DJ returns on the revolving stage playing upbeat records. This happens vice versa throughout the night.

Mark and Ray have just bought two cola's and are watching the girls dancing around their handbags on the huge dancefloor from the balcony.

"What do think ... should we try our luck?" asks Ray (Looks serious)

"Who with?" asks Mark (Looks concerned)

"What about those two, for a start" advises Ray (Points to dancefloor)

Ray pinpoints two slim girls, one blonde and the other

brunette.

"Well?" asks Ray (Looks serious)

"OK, but only if you lead the way, mate" replies Mark (Looks suspicious)

"Oh ... you're a bit of a scaredy cat they won't bite you" explains Ray (Smiles)

"OK then, I'll lead the way ... come on" replies Ray (Looks excited)

"Well, you are the oldest after all" adds Mark (Smiles)

"Yes, I suppose I am" laughs Ray

Keith, the General Manager passes by but stops to have a word with Mark and Ray ...

"Having a good time, lads?" asks Keith (Smiles)

"Oh yes, super thanks" replies Ray (Laughs)

"What do you think of the venue?" inquires Keith (Smiling)

"Excellent, top marks ... I can see us coming frequently here" replies Mark (Smiling)

"That's what I like to hear" adds Keith (Still smiling)

"So, it doesn't mecca you sick then?" asks Keith (Laughing)

Mark and Ray look at each other stunned ...

"That was a joke, boys ... get it mecca me sick?" asks Keith

Mark and Ray both laugh.

Suddenly, Mark and Ray notice someone familiar …

"Do you see who I see?" asks Mark (Looks shocked)

"It looks like …" adds Mark (Pointing)

"Who is it?" asks Ray (Looks puzzled)

"No, it can't be him" adds Mark (Looks stunned)

"Is it someone you know?" adds Ray

"I thought for a moment it looked like Father Shamus Rafferty from Church" explains Mark (Looks serious)

"What would a priest be doing here, Mark?" asks Ray (Sounds stunned)

"Maybe your mistaken?" adds Ray (Looks concerned)

"Yea, maybe I am, Ray" replies Mark (Still stunned)

The DJ is now playing the latest pop and Soul records …

The dance floor is jammed packed with Saturday night revelers …

Mark follows Ray to the edge of the dance floor, both eyeing up the talent on offer …

Mark and Ray have found the courage to ask to dance with a couple of girls they had spied upon from the upper balcony …

The music is now playing loudly …

Ray and Mark decide to make their move …

"It's now or never, mate … follow me" advises Ray (Smiling)

Mony... Mony is now playing, and the dance floor rapidly fills up ...

Ray and Mark decide to make their move ...

"Can I have this dance?" asks Ray (Smiling)

Mark follows suit ...

"Can I have this dance?" asks Mark (Smiling)

Both girls respond with friendly smiles ...

"Hi, I'm Ray" advises Ray (Smiling)

"Barbara ... my names Barbara" replies the slim brunette girl

"Hi, I'm Mark" adds Mark (blushing)

"Julie" replies the blonde slim girl

Both girls are in their teens wearing fluorescent blouses and miniskirts. Barbara is five foot 4, has long brunette hair, brown eyes.

Julie is also five foot 4, has long blonde hair with blue eyes.

Both girls are quite attractive ...

"Do you come here often?" asks Ray (Shouts above music)

Mark asks the same Question ...

Both girls seem to be interested and dance with Ray and Mark for a while ... but then decide to go off the floor ...

"We're going for a drink ... see you both later" advises

Barbara (Flashes a smile)

Mark is also flashed with a smile from Julie ...

Ray and Mark are suddenly left in the lurch ...

"See, I told you it wasn't going to be easy, Mark" advises Ray (Looks glum)

"There's as good a fish in the sea that ever came out of it, mate" replies Mark (Both Laughing)

"Don't worry ... we've got all the time in the World" adds Ray (Laughs)

"Yes, the World is our oyster" replies Mark (Both Laugh)

"Somehow, I've got a feeling that tonight is the night" explains Ray (Optimistic)

"I can feel it in my waters" adds Ray (Laughs)

"Stick with me kid ... our ships come in" advises Ray

"OK, if you say so" replies Mark (Looks stunned)

"Come on ... let's try our luck with another two girls" adds Ray

"OK, if you say so" advises Mark (Smiles)

"We're on a roll" laughs Ray

"Never say never" adds Mark (Both Laughing)

"I totally agree we should never rule anything or anyone for that matter, out" replies Ray

"W've got our reputations to think about" advises Mark

"What about those over there?" asks Ray

"Who are they?" asks Mark

"The next two of course" adds Ray

Both laughing ...

Mark and Ray go back on to the huge dancefloor and begin to chat up a couple of girls ...

"Do you come here often?" asks Mark

Ray laughs and gets into deep conversation ...

"Do you like doing the barn dance?" asks Ray

"No, I hate it" replies one of the girls

All laugh at Ray's opening lines ...

"Your both cool ... I will give you that" explains one of the girls

The DJ plays a mix of pop and Soul music ...

"This is more like it" advises Mark

SUMMERTIME CITY '75

Mark and Ray are now in their early twenties and are still ardent admirers of the Mecca Locarno in Manningham Lane, Bradford.

It is still the place to be, and Bobby Brook's Band are still resident at the iconic venue.

Will Mark and Ray find true love this summer?

Glam Rock is the music of the Seventies era along with Disco!

Iconic venues Batley Variety Club and the Sheffield Fiesta are part of the Seventies revolution in Cabaret style entertainment.

Worldwide stars would come to entertain the audiences.

Meanwhile for Mark and Ray it's yet another visit to the Mecca Locarno on Manningham Lane in Bradford.

Mark and Ray have gone for the long-haired look with sideburns to match.

Mark is wearing a power blue flared suit with 24-inch

bell bottoms, a white shirt with poke your eyes out collars, a kipper tie in all the colours of the rainbow and wearing platform shoes.

Ray has gone for the more reserved look in trademark corduroy green jacket, white shirt, and tie, black flared 27-inch bell bottoms and very modern up to date specs!

Ray meets Mark outside their familiar spot at Bradford Library ...

"Do you come here often?" greets Mark (Smiling)

"Only to meet you, mate" quips Ray (Both Laughing)

"Well, if we don't pull tonight, Mark" advises Ray (Smiles)

"I know ... I have a good feeling though tonight" replies Mark

"Why is someone touching you up?" laughs Ray

"You and your sense of humour ... one day it will get us both in trouble" advises Mark (Looks serious)

Ray and Mark start to walk away from the library and follow the road up to Manningham Lane. They walk past an old haunt ... THE HOLE IN THE WALL ... Tamla Motown can be heard blasting out!

They both eventually arrive early at the Mecca Locarno and are greeted by Keith, the General Manager, and the Bouncers on the door.

"You both look dressed to kill, tonight" advises Frank (Doorman)

Mark and Ray are both on good terms and are well known to Keith and the door staff.

Both have been going to the Mecca since its humble beginnings in the Swinging Sixties!

"We've got shares in this place" quips Ray (Smiling)

"That you do ... that you do" replies Keith (Smiles)

"If ever you two wanted a job here ... I will give you one" adds Keith

"Well, thank you, Keith ... we'll keep it in mind" replies Mark (Smiling)

"We need more young blood to keep the place fresh" advises Keith

All of this is taking place in the foyer inside the iconic venue!

Suddenly, two teenage girls turn up and ask for entry.

Mark and Ray are made aware when one of the girls gives them a flirtatious wink ...

"You could be in there tonight" advises Ray (Smiles)

"I thought she had something in her eye" replies Mark (Smiling)

"Come on ... are you green or what?" asks Ray (Looks serious)

"What?" adds Mark (Both laugh)

"OK, enough of the old jokes, mate" adds Ray (Laughs)

Mark and Ray leave the Foyer and enter the Stag Room. They both check their hair in the multi mirrored section then enter the ballroom.

In front of them is a glass case from floor to ceiling advertising the next special occasion ...

> *NEXT SATURDAY 8pm-1am*
> *BALI HAI DISCOTHEQUE ...*
> *PARTY NIGHT ...*
>
> *ADVANCE TICKETS ONLY ... THIS IS BOUND TO BE A SELL OUT!!!*

"Fancy going to that, Ray?" asks Mark (Looks enthusiastic)

"Yea, why not ... I will book our tickets later tonight" advises Ray (Smiles)

"I wonder what it means ... Bali Hai?" asks Mark (Looks inquisitive)

"It's a kind of Polynesian night" advises Ray (Smiling)

"You know a summery type of evening" adds Ray

"Gotcha" replies Mark (Looks pleased)

Mark and Ray then walk to the left of the showcase and enter the balcony that surrounds the Ballroom.

The Bobby Brook Band are playing the up-to-date latest music and lots of people are already on the dance floor.

Mark and Ray make their way down the stairs to the ground floor of the Ballroom.

The dance floor is immense, and it is great for dancing.

"Do you know what, Mark?" asks Ray (Looks serious)

"What, mate?" replies Mark (Looks stunned)

"You could lose yourself on that dance floor" advises Mark (Looks smug)

"Great" adds Mark (Smiling)

"Why great?" asks Ray (Looks puzzled)

"Well, if for instance you make a complete clot of yourself no one will notice" explains Mark (Smiling)

"Mmm ... we'll see" replies Ray (Looking completely baffled)

"Come on I'll treat you to a beer" advises Mark (Smiles)

Ray and Mark wander over to the stage at the end of the Ballroom.

The Band stops playing, and Bobby Brook makes an announcement ...

"OK everyone, it's time to take your partners for the Barn dance" advises Bobby (Smiling)

The Band are made up of several members on keyboards, drums, and various guitars. Bobby plays the trumpet and is obviously the Leader of the band. There are also three singers. Two females and a male ...

"Oh, no ... I am off" advises Mark (Looks serious)

"Well, I'm going to try it" replies Ray (Looks equally serious)

"Can you, do it?" asks Mark (Smiling)

"I'll soon find out" quips Ray (Laughs)

Both begin to laugh, and while Mark goes to the bar to order the beers ... Ray decides to step on to the dance floor where lots of people are joined in a ring!

After fifteen minutes an exhausted Ray returns to the side of the dance floor where Mark is waiting and hands him his beer ...

"Well, that nearly did me in Mark" advises Ray (Looks shattered)

"How come, Ray?" asks Mark (Looks serious)

"I didn't realise it was a change your partner dance" replies Ray (Looks stunned)

"That'll teach you" replies Mark (Laughs)

"I met some stunning girls though" adds Ray (Sounds serious)

"How did you get on?" asks Mark (Looks interested)

"They all asked me if I had a mate" explains Ray (Looks serious)

"Why?" adds Mark (Looks baffled)

"I'll give you three guesses" advises Ray (Winks)

"We could have cracked it tonight, mate" adds Ray

"Shall we try our luck?" asks Mark (Looks excited)

"OK ... wait for the music to change to records" advises Ray

The Bobby Brook Band begin to play "Time is Tight" and the revolving stage changes back to the DJ playing records.

Hits of the day ring out followed by various Soul hits ...

Mark and Ray notice two girls dancing together on the dance floor ...

"Come on Mark let's try those two over there" advises Ray (Points)

Both girls are brunette and dressed in the fashions of the day ...

"OK ... but you lead the way" replies Mark (Looks shy)

"Scaredy cat ... they won't bite you" adds Ray (Laughs)

Mark and Ray venture on to the dance floor.

There are lots of girls in pairs dancing around their handbags.

Ray makes his move followed by Mark ...

"Can I have this dance, love?" asks Ray (Smiles)

"Yea ... why not?" reply both girls (Smiling)

Mark moves closer to her friend ...

"What about you?" asks the other girl (Smiles)

"May I ..." asks Mark (Looks shy)

"Yes, of course" replies the other girl (Big Smile)

"My name is Mary" advises the girl (Still smiling)

"Mark, I'm Mark" replies Mark (Looks embarrassed)

Mary is five foot 4, wearing a navy-blue boiler type overall and a white flowing blouse. She has wavy brunette hair, green eyes and attractive ...

Ray is dancing with Mandy ...

Mandy is five foot 6, has brown hair, hazel eyes and wearing a fashionable maxi dress with a white blouse ...

"Do you come here often?" asks Ray (Sounds cheesy)

"No ... we're new ... aren't we Mary?" replies Mandy (Smiling)

Mary smiles and continues to dance with Mark ...

"You're a bit of a shy one, aren't you?" asks Mary (Smiling)

"Well, I ..." replies Mark (Lost for words)

"Don't worry ... I had my eye on you in the foyer" adds Mary (Winks)

"Really ... how?" asks Mark (Looks suspicious)

"We noticed you and your mate as we came in" replies Mary (Looks serious)

"Don't you remember I flashed a smile at you and winked?" asks Mary (Smiling)

"No ... wait a minute ... the girl in the foyer?" replies Mark (Looks shy)

"Yes, that was me, love" replies Mary (Laughs)

"You were talking to the General Manager and the door men" adds Mary

"Yes, that was us" replies Mark (Smiles)

Ray and Mandy decide to move off the dance floor.

"We're going for a drink" advises Ray (Winks)

"OK, see you in a little bit" replies Mark (Smiles)

"What about us?" asks Mary (Looks seductive)

"Us?" asks Mark (Sounds stunned)

"You and me" replies Mary (Flashes another smile)

"My, you really are shy, aren't you?" asks Mary (Looks serious)

The music suddenly changes to a smooch ...

"Fancy getting close up?" asks Mary (Smiling)

"Yea, why not" replies Mark (Smiles)

Several slow dances later, Mark and Mary get closer ...

"You don't take advantage of a girl, do you?" asks Mary (Looks concerned)

"Sorry, I'm kind of new to all of this, Mary" replies Mark (Looks shy)

"I wonder what Ray and Mandy are up to?" asks Mary (Looks serious)

Mark and Mary, walk off the dance floor hand in hand ...

They come across Ray and Mandy snogging at a

nearby table.

"Boy he's a fast worker" advises Mary (Looks stunned)

Ray and Mandy come up for breath laughing ...

"I was wondering when you'd show up" advises Ray (Smiling)

"Can we join you?" asks Mary (Smiles)

"What in a snog?" asks Mandy (Laughs)

"Sure, of course you can" replies Ray (Laughing)

Mary and Mark sit at the table together ...

Mary decides to go in for the kill and both she and Mark end up snogging the face off each other ...

"Well, at last" advises Ray (Claps)

"I was beginning to think you didn't have it in you" adds Ray (Smiling)

"Come on Mandy ... let's leave those two love birds on their own for a while" laughs Ray (Winks)

Ray and Mandy move away from the table hand in hand ...

Mary and Mark continue where they left off ...

Mark decides to ask Mary out on a date ...

"What are you doing tomorrow?" asks Mark (Smiles)

"Why ... are you asking me out on a date?" replies Mary (Smiling)

"Yes, of course I am ... why not?" adds Mark (Smiling)

"What have you got in mind, Mark?" asks Mary (Looks

excited)

"Maybe a trip into Leeds by train" explains Mark

"Then we can take in ten pin bowling" adds Mark (Looks serious)

"That sounds like a lot of fun" replies Mary (Still smiling)

"You can ask Mandy and Ray to join us if you want" advises Mark

"No love, it will be just you and me" beams Mary (Starts Kissing)

Mark suddenly looks round the now packed Ballroom and thinks he notices someone familiar ...

"Why it's ..." advises Mark (Looks serious)

"No, it can't be" adds Mark (Sounds stunned)

"Who is it, Mark?" asks Mary (Looks around)

"Father Rafferty" explains Mark (Looks stunned)

"What would a priest be doing here, Mark?" asks Mary

"What indeed?" replies Mark (Looks puzzled)

Ray and Mandy return, hand in hand to rejoin Mary and Mark ...

"Hello ... come up for a breather, have we?" laughs Ray

Mark turns red in the face!

"Oh, look he's blushing" adds Mandy (Smiling) (Arm round Mark)

"Leave Mark alone" replies Mary (Looks concerned)

Mark advises Ray that he has seen someone familiar on the prowl in the Ballroom ...

"Guess who I've just seen?" asks Mark (Looks serious)

"Who?" asks Ray (Looks stunned)

"Father Rafferty" adds Mark (Sounds concerned)

"What here again?" adds Ray (Sounds stunned)

"Why would a Roman Catholic priest want to come here?" asks Ray

"Maybe he is leading a double life" adds Mandy (Looks serious)

"Yea, maybe he is" replies Mary

"Whatever it is ... it all looks mighty suspicious" replies Mark (Looks stunned)

"Who knows what they get up to when they are on their own" adds Mark

LOVE CHEAT

Mark and Mary go on their first date ten pin bowling in Leeds.

Ray and Mandy decide to go on a visit to the cinema, and the back row in particular!

A Love Cheat is exposed ... and it ends up all over the national newspapers!

Mecca Locarno, Bradford ... 10am Keith Forbes (General Manager) office ...

Keith is at his desk looking through lots of paperwork when suddenly the phone rings ...

"Yes, Jean" replies Keith (Smiles)

"I have a BBC producer on Line One for you Keith" advises Jean

"OK, put him through, Jean" replies Keith (Sounds stunned)

Jean immediately transfers the call the Keith ...

"Keith Forbes, General Manager ... how can I help you?" asks Keith (Sounds serious)

"Howard Prentice, BBC Television programming"

advises the voice

"How can I help you, Howard?" asks Keith (Sounds stunned)

"We would like to host a show at your venue" explains the producer

"What kind of show?" asks Keith (Sounds excited)

"An edition and heat for COME DANCING" adds the producer

"Please call me Howard" replies the producer (Sounds sincere)

"It sounds very intriguing, Howard" adds Keith (Still stunned)

"How will it all work?" asks Keith (Looks concerned)

"Our Research Team will be in touch with regards to dates for transmission" explains Howard (Sounds serious)

"We will commit ourselves to your wishes" replies Keith

"I will just have to clear it with Head Office" explains Keith (Sounds serious)

"There's no need to do that Keith ... we have already been in contact with Mr. Morley, and he has given the go ahead" explains the producer

"Would Wednesday be OK for rehearsals and transmission?" asks Howard (Sounds serious)

"What this week?" asks Keith (Sounds stunned)

"We thought about next week" explains the producer

"OK, Howard... that will be fine" replies Keith (Sounds excited)

"Our Team will be in contact with you soon" explains Howard

Meanwhile, Mark and Mary are having their first date at Leeds Tenpin Bowling in the Merrion Centre ...

The venue has 26 bowling lanes, an arcade, table tennis and pool tables. It is the place to be for entertainment in Leeds, and it is situated opposite the Cinderella/Rockafella discotheque.

Mary and Mark collect their bowling shoes from the kiosk and begin to change from their own shoes ...

"I'm not really very good at this, Mark" advises Mary (Looks serious)

"Don't worry about that, Mary ... I am a bit of a learner too" explains Mark (Laughs)

"We're just playing for fun, Mary" adds Mark (Smiling)

Mary takes aim with her first bowl and manages to clear all the pins in the first run!

"Lucky shot" advises Mary (Smiling)

Mark bowls and it goes nowhere!

"Not to worry ... if I can't beat you at bowling what about a snog" replies Mark (Smiling)

"You get ten out of ten for that, love" adds Mary (Both snogging)

Ray and Mandy are taking in the latest film at one of the cinemas in the Centre of Leeds ...

Back seat lovers ...

"This is the place" advises Ray (Smiling)

"Hey ... no hanky panky, Ray" replies Mandy (Sounds serious)

"As if I would" adds Ray (Laughs)

Meanwhile, back in Bradford news of a story and scandal hitting the headlines concerning ... Father Shamus Rafferty!

It is all over the news on television and on "A" boards in Leeds and Bradford.

Mark and Mary leave the Merrion Centre and notice the headlines ...

"Isn't young love wonderful?" shout a couple of drunks

Mark and Mary both look embarrassed!

Mark and Mary go red in the face.

Mark notices the headlines on the "A" board and the all too familiar photograph!

"I know that man" advises Mark (Looks serious)

"Which man?" asks Mary (Looks around)

"Not those two drunks ... the face in the A board" replies Mark (Looks embarrassed)

"Who is it?" asks Mary (Looks concerned)

"It's Father Shamus" adds Mark (Looks sad)

"Who?" adds Mary (Looks stunned)

"He's a priest from Bradford" explains Mark

Mark decides to buy the latest edition of the Evening Post newspaper ...

"My God ... what a scandal" advises Mark (Looks concerned)

"Why, what has he been up to?" asks Mary (Looks serious)

"It looks like he married a former parishioner, had two children with her and obviously hid it from the Church authorities" explains Mark

"The newspaper advises ... court case pending" adds Mark

"Well, I guess it proves he's only human" replies Mary

"But they are also linking that rape case of a 17-year-old girl in the same era" advises Mark

"He has gone a step too far though" adds Mark

Ray and Mandy are enjoying their time at the cinema and decide to meet up again on Sunday.

Mark and Mary continue their date also vowing to meet again on Sunday.

Next day, Mark meets up with Ray prior to their dates with Mary and Mandy.

"Well, Mark ... how did you get on with Mary on your first date?" asks Ray (Looks serious)

"It was great fun ...we decided to go ten pin bowling in Leeds" replies Mark (Smiles)

"What about you, Ray ... how did you get on with Mandy?" asks Mark (Looks inquisitive)

"It was a back seat at the cinema date" laughs Ray

"That sounds like you" replies Mark (Smiling)

"We're meeting up later" adds Ray (Looks excited)

"What about you and Mary?" asks Ray (Looks concerned)

"We're also meeting up later" advises Mark (Smiling)

Back at the Mecca Locarno in Bradford ... Keith Forbes is briefing his back-room staff with regards a big occasion at the venue ...

All staff are attending the meeting in the Boardroom ...

"Please sit down everyone" advises Keith (Looks serious)

"I've got some exciting news" adds Keith

All staff are now sat around the Boardroom table awaiting Keith's update ...

"We've been chosen as a venue for the BBC Television series COME DANCING" advises Keith (Looks excited)

All the staff are taken by surprise at Keith's announcement!

"It appears we are perfectly situated, and Friday will be the recording of what may be the first of many programmes here in Bradford" explains Keith (Smiling)

"Will we get to meet Terry Wogan?" asks Jean (Looks excited)

"We will all get to meet him, Jean" advises Keith (Smiling)

"Will we need extra security?" ask Mike and Pete (Doormen)

"If we do, we'll ask for reinforcements from Leeds and York" explains Keith (Looks confident)

"Has it been cleared by Head Office, Keith?" asks Derek (Looks concerned)

"Everything's been cleared by Head Office and Mr. Morley in particular" advises Keith (Looks serious)

"What do we have to do?" asks Jean (Looks concerned)

"Just be yourselves ... be smart in your uniform on the night" adds Keith (Smiles)

"What about meeting Terry?" asks Jean (Looks star struck)

"You'll all get plenty of opportunities to meet and talk to Terry during the day on Friday" explains Keith (Laughs)

"When do they start recording?" asks Bill (Lighting Manager)

"We've been told cameras will roll at 7.30pm, Bill" explains Keith (Looks serious)

Derek is asked to brief everyone concerning matters on the dance floor ...

"We're hosting two teams of Ballroom dancers in a heat for the finals in London" explains Derek (Looks serious)

Bobby Brook and Jackie enter the meeting ...

"Bob, you and the Band will be our resident musicians, as always, on the night" advises Keith (Smiling)

"We've already been briefed by the BBC and what music to play" advises Bobby (Smiles)

"I will be singing too" explains Jackie (Laughs)

Meanwhile, Mark and Ray intend to take Mary and Mandy to the BBC transmission/recording evening at Bradford Mecca Locarno.

"Well girls are you interested in going to the BBC Television recording at the Mecca on Friday?" asks Ray (Looks enthusiastic)

"No, not really" replies Mandy (Looks glum)

"Why?" asks Mark (Looks puzzled)

"It will be all ballroom dancing ... we would rather come here this week" advises Mary (Big Smile)

Mark, Ray, Mary, and Mandy are having coffee in the Continental Cafe on Godwin Street in Bradford.

The downstairs basement area is known as THE HOLE IN THE WALL.

It is a teenager's haunt selling coca cola and has pin

ball machines to play.

The dancing area is entered through a hole in the wall, but the most amazing Soul music is played there ... and when you come out your ears are ringing!

"We would love to come here on Friday" advises Mary (Smiling)

"What do you think?" asks Ray (Looks excited)

"Yea, why not" replies Mark (Looks equally excited)

"OK ... are you up for it too, Mandy?" asks Ray

"Yes, count me in, Ray" replies Mandy (Smiling)

"Friday night, it is then" promises Mark

"It's a date" reply Mary and Mandy (Both smiling)

Developments and a Court Case hearing are now brought against Catholic Priest and Love Cheat, Shamus Rafferty!

It appears that Rafferty, who is in his late forties, is also up for groping a girl of 17 in his parish in Bradford.

The Crown Prosecution Service are bringing a case against him for this.

It also turns out that Rafferty was secretly married for over ten years!

Reporting and speculation are rife.

It is an old story ... Rafferty used to go to the Mecca Locarno dance hall in Bradford on his days off!

No one knew about his double life except his so-called

wife who kept their relationship a secret.

Rafferty used to say mass at weekends then spend the rest of the week with his wife and children in Yeadon!

What a scandal!

Mark, Mary, Ray, and Mandy meet up on Friday as arranged and go to THE HOLE IN THE WALL which is adjacent to the Continental Coffee House.

It costs pennies for entry, and you can make a cola last all night if you want to.

The records are played loud, and it is a very intimate venue in a cellar type atmosphere which runs across two rooms.

Ray orders four colas at the bar. Fluorescent mauve lighting fills the ceiling and dance floor.

Mary, Mark, Ray, and Mandy step out on to the dance floor which is packed with many other dancers.

Back at the Mecca Locarno in Manningham Lane Jean bumps into Terry Wogan ahead of the COME DANCING recordings ...

"Sorry about that ... please accept my apologies" advises a voice

Jean turns round to see that its Terry Wogan and is stunned!

"Why, it's you Terry" mumbles Jean (Looks surprised)

"... and you are?" asks Terry (Smiling)

"My names Jean ... I am the receptionist ... lovely to

meet you, Terry" replies Jean (Looks star truck)

"You're the most important person in the building, Jean" quips Terry (With a glint in his eye)

"Am I ... why, Terry?" asks Jean (Looks stunned)

"You're the first person everyone meets ... lovely to meet you, Jean" adds Terry (Smiling)

Jean is stunned and kisses Terry on the cheek ...

"What was that for, Jean?" asks a stunned Terry

"A kiss for luck and a welcome to Bradford" adds Jean (Smiling)

With a twinkle in his eye ... Terry takes to the floor in his black tuxedo to open the proceedings!

BOBBY AND JACKIE'S STORY

Bobby Brook and his Band are resident musicians at the Mecca Locarno Ballroom in Bradford.

Jackie is also one of the resident singers in the band.

Bobby and Jackie's story is a chequered one to say the least!

LIVE TRANSMISSION OF THE BBC TELEVISION SERIES ... COME DANCING

Host TERRY WOGAN, Resident musicians, BOBBY BROOK BAND.

A BBC Floor Manager gives the OK for the "live" show ...

A countdown begins ...

3-2-1 ...Action/Green Lit/Transmission ...

The BBC credits make way for the new era of

entertainment ...

The cameras all lead on to the main stage ...

"Good evening and welcome" greets Host, Terry Wogan (Smiles)

Bobby Brook is already in place on stage in the Orchestra section with his Band.

Backing Singers, Shirley, Jackie, and Tom are ready for the first number to be played.

A BBC Producer is on hand for transmission ...

Terry Wogan introduces both teams competing in the heat ...

The Northeast and the Southwest.

Everyone loves the "offbeat" section and can relate to it.

Bobby turns to Jackie ...

"All set, Jackie?" asks Bobby (Smiles)

"As ready as we will ever be, Bobby" replies Jackie (Smiling)

"No on the night nerves?" asks Bobby (Looks concerned)

"Only a few butterflies" replies Tom (Smiling)

"Butterflies?" asks Bobby (Looks puzzled)

"In our tummies" replies Shirley (Smiling)

"Don't worry that's natural ... just go for it" advises Bobby (Laughs)

Meanwhile, Keith Forbes (General Manager) is overwhelmed by just how many people have turned up!

Keith and the door attendants are really having a night of it.

Reporters from the Telegraph and Argus in Bradford are on hand to snap the ballroom dancers in all their glory marking the exciting time for the Mecca Locarno in Bradford.

Ray, Mandy, Mark, and Mary are at the famous HOLE IN THE WALL in Godwin Street ...

It is a mods paradise, except news is coming in of a raid by Rockers on their motorbikes!

Mods and Rockers are two conflicting British youth cultures.

Mods are famous for wearing fine Italian suits and parkas. They ride around on Lambretta scooters.

Rockers are greasy leather wearing motor cyclists and are hard as nails Rock n Roll enthusiasts.

"Something is brewing" advises Ray (Looks serious)

"How do you know?" asks Mary (Looks concerned)

"There's a feeling of anxiety here" replies Ray

"What do you think?" asks Mark (Looks serious)

"I think we had better split with the girls, before it gets heavy" advises Ray (Looks concerned)

Mark, Mary, Ray, and Mandy manage to make their

way up the flight of stairs away from the crowded basement. They notice the Rockers congregating on their bikes just up the road.

All four head downhill into Bradford away from the pending trouble. They are now outside the Odeon Cinema next to the Alhambra Theatre.

A sudden crash bang fills the air!

A couple of the Rockers have kicked over several scooters and lambrettas parked outside the Hole in the Wall!

Pandemonium prevails.

The Police arrive at the scene and collar a few individuals...

"Boy, did we just get out of there in time?" asks Mark (Looks stunned)

Bobby Brook and Jackie go back a long way!

When Bobby started out, he brought Jackie into the Band almost immediately.

Bobby and Jackie were once childhood school sweethearts!

Bobby recalls his memories...

"We first met at just nine years old in school" advises Bobby (Smiles)

"We have remained great friends ever since" adds Bobby

"Yet you didn't marry ... why?" asks Keith (Looks

serious)

"We felt it would have ruined our relationship if we had committed to marriage" explains Booby (Looks sincere)

"But because we work together in the band it's as if she's my second wife" advises Bobby (Smiling)

"And your first wife?" asks a stunned Keith

"Why, music of course" explains Bobby (Looks serious)

Jackie walks in on the conversation ...

"Are you both talking about me?" asks Jackie (Laughs)

"I was just explaining to Keith how we became such good friends" replies Bobby (Smiles)

"I bet Bobby didn't tell you how he dumped me, Keith" adds Jackie (Looks serious)

Keith and Bobby both looked shocked ...

"Well, he did, didn't you Bobby?" advises Jackie (Looks daggers)

"Well, I ..." fumbles Bobby (Looks sheepish)

"Why?" asks Keith (Looks concerned)

"He was unable to fully commit Keith that's why" explains Jackie (Looks serious)

"Really, Bob?" replies Keith (Looks shocked)

"Yes, I'm afraid it's true" advises Bobby (Looks stunned)

"Still, we're best friends now, and it works" adds Jackie (Smiles)

"We've got the best of both Worlds" explains Bobby (Smiling)

The COME DANCING event is nearing completion of transmission and it receives a welcome response from the BBC and its viewers drawing on a large audience.

"I've just had Head Office on the phone" advises Keith (Smiling)

"Was it good news, Keith?" asks Jackie (Looks serious)

"The BBC want to do more COME DANCING programmes from our Ballroom here in Bradford" replies Keith (Looks excited)

"That's wonderful news, Keith" advises Booby (Looks equally excited)

"Well, I think we should celebrate" adds Jackie (Smiling)

"Good idea, Jackie" explains Keith (Looks stunned)

Keith decides to throw a Party Night at the venue in the coming weeks as a thank you to all staff and all concerned with the Mecca!

"We will be working though" advises Bob (Smiles)

"Well, as resident Band you and Jackie can throw a large party" explains Keith

"We will obviously invite members of the public too, and they can take part in our Big News Event" adds Keith (Smiling)

Jackie and Bobby leave Keith's office and begin to chat ...

"You know Keith was right" advises Bobby (Smiles)

"Right about what, Bobby?" asks Jackie (Smiling)

"Why didn't we marry?" adds Bobby (Sounds serious)

"Don't start that again ... you know why" replies Jackie (Looks serious)

"Anyway, you're a happily married man" explains Jackie

"I wouldn't exactly say happy" replies Bobby (Looks concerned)

"Well, you know what your mother would have said to that don't you?" adds Jackie

"No, what would she say?" asks Bobby (Looks inquisitive)

"You've made your bed ... now lie in it" explains Jackie (Looks serious)

"Oh, yea ... she would" replies Bobby (Looks sad)

"Come on, Bobby ... let's get back to rehearsals" explains Jackie

Mark, Ray, Mary, and Mandy are ready for another night out ...

"Well, where do you fancy going?" asks Ray (Looks serious)

"What about a trip to the seaside?" asks Mary (Looks excited)

"Good idea, Mary" replies Mary (Smiling)

"Yea, I'm up for it too" adds Mandy (Smiles)

"I've got an interview on Monday" explains Mary (Looks serious)

"Where?" asks Mark (Looks equally serious)

"St Lukes Hospital" advises Mary (Looks excited)

"Why what's wrong with you?" asks Ray (Looks concerned)

"Nothing is wrong with me ... I am planning to be a Nurse" adds Mary

"A Nurse?" asks Mandy (Looks stunned)

"Well yea ... why not?" asks Mary (Looks puzzled)

Mark and Ray buy the train tickets at the Central Station for Blackpool ...

"OK, Blackpool ... here we come" shouts Ray (Laughs)

Mark is more reserved and still in shock with Mary's announcement.

Ray, Mandy, Mary, and Mark all board the waiting train bound for Blackpool.

Ray pulls Mark to one side ...

"We've only known them five minutes and you've come over all serious" advises Ray (Looks concerned)

"Just play it cool, Mark" explains Ray (Looks serious)

"Yea, your right, Ray" replies Mark (Laughs)

Mary and Mandy settle back in a closed

compartment ... Mark and Ray look for the buffet car ...

Back in Bradford the Court Case is starting to build against Father Shamus Rafferty.

Television and Newspaper restrictions are in place due to the intense pressure on the victim to come forward.

It is a time when a certain Yorkshire Ripper appears on the scene.

JULY 1977 ... Maureen Long was coming out of the Mecca Locarno in Bradford when she was offered a lift home by an unknown man.

That man was Peter Sutcliffe.

He attempted to murder Maureen but luckily a passerby found her.

She was barely alive and suffered memory loss because of the attack.

A week later, the Police set up several desks in the Foyer of the Mecca Locarno venue in Bradford.

Mark, Mary, Ray, and Mandy are on their way in.

Keith Forbes (General Manager) greets them all on arrival ...

"Don't worry ... just co-operate with the Police Officers ... tell them what you know" advises Keith (Looks serious)

Mandy is known to several officers as she works for the Administration Section in Bradford.

"This way" advises a Police Officer (Looks serious)

"Name and address, please" asks another officer at a desk

All four give their names and addresses as requested to the officers.

"Were you here at the Locarno, last Friday?" asks a Police officer (Looks serious)

"Sorry, No" reply Mark and Ray (Look serious)

"OK, you can go in" advises the Police officer

Mary and Mandy are also cleared and follow them into the venue.

The Ballroom is now quite full, and Ray notices a woman on the dance floor.

It's a Policewoman dressed as Maureen Long in a dark wig ...

"What's going on?" asks Mary (Looks concerned)

"She is dressed as the victim, presumably to jog memories" advises Mark (Looks serious)

The reign of the Yorkshire Ripper affected all our lives back then.

It was a time when girls and women were unsafe and one never to be forgotten!

PARTY NIGHT

Keith Forbes (General Manager) puts on a party to remember at the Mecca Locarno in Bradford!

Mary has good news for Mark. Ray and Mandy's romance is on the rocks!

News of a COME DANCING Special!

Thursday ... 2 days before PARTY NIGHT at Bradford Mecca Locarno ...

Mark meets Mary in Bradford on Wednesday evening ...

"So, what do you fancy doing tonight, Mary?" asks Mark (Smiles)

"What about a drink and the cinema?" replies Mary (Smiling)

"That's a good idea" adds Mark

"I have also got some news to tell you" advises Mary (Looks serious)

"What news?" asks Mark (Looks concerned)

"I will tell you all about it in the pub" explains Mary (Looks coy)

Meanwhile, Ray and Mandy are going through a rough patch ...

Ray calls Mandy on the telephone ...

"See, I told you I had to work tonight" advises Mandy

Ray is not so pleased, especially as they decided on this date several nights ago!

"Why tonight?" asks Ray (Sounds suspicious)

"Sorry, I can't get out of it ... see you at the weekend" replies Mandy

Back at the Mecca Locarno on Manningham Lane, Keith Forbes is talking to Bobby Brook and the singers on the dance floor ...

"So, Bob ... what are we in for tonight?" asks Keith (Smiles)

"I thought, as it was Party Night, we would throw in some reggae and have a sort of competition" advises Bobby

"What kind of competition?" asks Keith (Looks serious)

"Maybe a limbo dancing one ... how low can you go, you know?" replies Bobby

"Well, it all sounds like fun, Bob" adds Keith

"We've also been asked by the Telegraph and Argus to find a girl in a 100 contest" explains Bobby

"That's OK ... but I'm not so sure about the limbo" advises Keith

"Your right, I don't fancy showing off my modesty" laughs Jackie

"All those girls in miniskirts" adds Keith (Ponders)

"No ... sorry we must keep it clean, remember we've got a reputation to live up to now we are on Come Dancing" explains Keith (Looks serious)

"Sorry, we will have to knock the limbo on the head, Bobby" orders Keith

"OK, you're the Boss" replies Bobby (Looks sad)

"What about our next Come Dancing appearance?" asks Bobby

"We've been asked to stage a Special in the autumn followed by several heat appearances in the next series" advises Keith (Looks excited)

"OK, we will have a full rehearsal tomorrow afternoon then on Saturday it's the real thing" adds Keith (Sounds serious)

Meanwhile, Mark and Mary are settling in a cozy corner of a city Centre pub ...

"Well, Mary ... what's your news?" asks Mark (Looks serious)

"I've been accepted as a Student Nurse at Saint Lukes" advises Mary (Sounds serious)

Mark is stunned but Mary is extremely excited at the news ...

"Saint Lukes?" replies Mark (Looks concerned)

"It's only a short walk-up Little Horton Lane" explains Mary

"And I can live in" adds Mary (Looks serious)

"Live in?" replies Mark (Looks stunned)

"Yes, in the Nurses Quarters" advises Mary

Saint Lukes Hospital is a grade 2 listed complex.

Meanwhile, Ray is thinking of changing his job and girl friend at the same time!

Ray phones Mark and tells him the news about Mandy ... and Mark advises she is the news!

"What they are both Nurses?" asks Ray (Sounds serious)

"Mary is just about to become a Student Nurse at Saint Lukes" advises Mark (Sounds concerned)

"Looks like we may have to return to our old stomping ground" advises Ray

"Why?" asks Mark (Sounds puzzled)

"You will soon find out" advises Ray (Laughs)

"We're both on a downer" adds Ray (Sounds serious)

"What downer?" asks Mark (Sounds puzzled)

"We're on the road to nowhere with those two" explains Ray

"Yea, maybe your right" replies Mark (Looks sad)

"Always remember keep your options open" insists Ray (Laughs)

"Next thing you will know is that they will be working all the shifts under the sun" explains Ray (Sounds serious)

"What shifts?" asks Mark (Looks puzzled)

"Sadly, they are both shift workers ... and going out with them long term is not a good prospect at all, Mark" adds Ray

"No, mate ... what we need is fresh blood" advises Ray (Laughs)

"But I like Mary" replies Mark (Sounds serious)

"Listen Mark believe me before you know it, she will dump you" explains Ray

"Why?" asks Mark (Sounds serious)

"Because you will no longer conform to her way of life and the shift pattern" advises Ray

"You will have to dump her one way or another" explains Ray

"Why ... have you dumped Mandy?" asks Mark

"Maybe" replies Ray (Sounds coy)

"Either you have, or you haven't" replies Mark (Sounds concerned)

"You will thank me for this" explains Ray (Looks serious)

"Will I?" asks Mark (Sounds intrigued)

"Yes, of course you will" adds Ray

"Believe me, Mark ... taking out shift workers is a

clear recipe for problems in the future" explains Ray (Sounds serious)

"OK, Ray ... I hear you loud and clear and I agree" replies Mark

Back at the Mecca Locarno on Manningham Lane it's PARTY NIGHT FRIDAY ...

Keith has asked for a notice board to be put outside the entrance to the venue ...

Keith is in conversation with all staff in the meeting room ...

"Well, what do you think?" asks Keith (Sounds serious)

The notice reads ...

MECCA DANCING,

LOCARNO, BRADFORD

THE "IN" PLACE TO BE

YOU DON'T HAVE TO LIVE IN BRADFORD TO GET THE VIP TREATMENT

DON'T JUST LISTEN TO THE GOOD STORIES ABOUT THE

EVERLASTING LOVE

LOCARNO, BRADFORD

COME AND SEE FOR YOURSELF!

WE WELCOME ANYBODY AND EVERYBODY WHO LIKES A GOOD TIME AND YOU WILL GET IT AT THE LOCARNO, BRADFORD!

PRESENTS ...

THIS FRIDAY – PARTY NIGHT 8PM TILL 1AM

LATE TRANSPORT AVAILABLE

BE SURE TO COME EARLY!!!

"It sounds like a great night, Keith" advises Tony (One of the Bar Managers)

"It will be busy though" adds Tony (Looks concerned)

"Well, that's what we want" replies Keith (Looks serious)

"Head Office has asked us to pull out all the stops particularly as we are now in the run up to being on BBC COME DANCING again" advises Keith (Looks excited)

"It's an exciting time for Bradford Mecca" adds Keith

"We've also got a new line up for all our other evening programmes during the week" explains Keith (Looks serious)

Bobby Brook knocks and enters the meeting room ...

"Late again as per usual, Bobby" quips Keith (Smiles)

"Sorry Keith ... I had to drop the missis off" replies Bobby (Smiling)

"We are just going through the new weekly programme of events here at the Locarno" explains Keith (Looks serious)

Keith hands out flyers to his staff ...

It reads ... LETS GO DANCING!

*OUTSTANDING BANDS,
COURTESY AND SERVICE,
ALL VISITORS WELCOME ...*

*RECORD NIGHT –
MONDAY – TOP DJ*

*NON-STOP DANCING
– EVERY EVENING*

OVER 21 NIGHT – EVERY WEDNESDAY

NIGHTLY (EXCEPT MONDAYS) DANCING TO BOBBY BROOK AND HIS BIG BAND

"I see I got a mention" laughs Bobby

"Yea, but the Singer's didn't" adds Jean (Looks puzzled)

"Sorry, that was an oversight" advises Keith (Looks apologetic)

"We will rectify that in our next flyer" explains Keith

"It helps if regulars know who our resident singers are" advises Bobby

"Yes, I totally agree with you, Bobby ... and as I said we will change that next time" assures Keith (Smiles)

It is fast approaching 8pm ... the DJ and Bobby Brook's Band are in place on the revolving stage.

Keith and the door attendants are in the Foyer waiting to greet and welcome dancers and new customers to the Mecca Ballroom.

There is a line of people snaking its way around the venue.

Suddenly, the doors open ...

"OK, please enter in an orderly manner" asks Derek

(One of the door attendants)

Keith is on hand to oversee and greet everyone coming into the prestigious venue ...

Mark and Ray are in the queue ...

Both are wearing fashionable attire ...

Mark is stopped by one of the door attendants ...

"Sorry you're not wearing a jacket" advises Mike (Another door attendant)

"You can't come in" adds Derek (Looks serious)

"It's a safari jacket" explains Mark (Looks concerned)

"Well, you're not on safari here" replies Frank (Looks serious)

Keith (General Manager) intervenes and allows Mark to enter the Locarno!

"Just remember to wear a proper jacket next time" advises Keith (Smiles)

"Thanks, Keith ... I promise I will" replies Mark (Looks relieved)

"I really did think this was OK" adds Mark (Looks serious)

"It's OK, lad ... you and your mate are regulars ... we need people like you" laughs Keith

Inside the Ballroom it is already beginning to fill up.

Mark and Ray head to the bar but suddenly notice Mandy and Mary sitting on some other boy's laps having their photos taken in an embrace!

"When I say cheese" advises a boy (Smiling)

"Don't forget to smile" adds another boy (Laughs)

"Why it's Mandy and Mary" advises Ray (Looks stunned)

"Yea, with another two blokes" replies Mark (Looks intrigued)

"Who's the love cheats now?" asks Ray (Looking daggers)

"Come on, Mark ... two can play that game" advises Ray

"Where are we going?" asks Mark (Sounds naive)

Ray and Mark head on to the packed dance floor where records are now being played by the resident DJ ...

"May we have this dance?" asks Ray (Smiles)

Both join two stunning brunettes on the dance floor.

"Yea, why not, love" replies one of the girls (Big Smile)

"I'm Stacey" introduces one of the girls (Smiling)

"Ray" replies Ray (Smiles)

Mark is more polite ...

"Do you come here often?" asks Mark (Smiles)

"Maybe" replies the second girl (Laughs)

"I'm Samantha" replies the second girl (Big Smile)

"Mark" (Looks serious)

"I like your gear" advises Samantha (Beaming)

"Are you on safari?" asks Stacey (Smiling)

"What in Bradford?" replies Mark (Laughs)

Ray joins in the banter ...

"Yea ... perhaps we are, love" explains Ray (All Laughing)

NEW YEAR'S EVE BALL

It's the end of the year and Keith Forbes (General Manager) at the Bradford Mecca Locarno has a special night lined up!

Mark and Ray make up with Mandy and Mary ... but is it too good to be true ... and will it last?

New Year's Eve ... 5 hours before Event ...

Rehearsals are taking place in the Ballroom ...

"We're making tonight's programme a family event" advises Keith (Sounds serious)

"Do you want us to play lots of party music, Keith?" asks Bobby

"Yes, especially party music" replies Keith (Smiling)

"What about me?" asks DJ Martin (Laughs)

"You will set the party atmosphere" advises Keith (Smiles)

"Play a mix of Jive, Ballroom ... all mixed together" adds Keith

"Also pop, upbeat festive tracks and party classics to say goodbye to the old year" explains Keith (Looks excited)

"You will both bring in the New Year celebrations" adds Keith

"Do you want a countdown to Big Ben?" asks Bobby (Looks serious)

"Yes, and memorable hits on the run up to it" advises Keith

"We want everyone in the Locarno to be in party mood and have a good time" explains Keith (Smiles)

"All bars will be open ... we have an extended license" adds Keith

"What about dress code?" asks Derek (One of the door attendants)

"Dress code is smart, expect party hats, fancy dress, party poppers, streamers" instructs Keith (Smiling)

"Don't exclude anyone without a tie or if they are wearing an usual jacket" orders Keith (Looks serious)

"Make everyone welcome ... we want it to be a night to remember" advises Keith (Smiling)

"Bring on the ball" replies Jean (Smiling)

"All tickets have now been sold" advises Keith (Looks pleased)

"What about on the door entry?" asks Derek (Looks sombre)

"I will be working it with you tonight" explains Keith

"We will meet and greet everyone" adds Keith (Smiles)

"We can let in another 50 or so on the door" advises Keith

"I will tell you when we are at capacity" adds Keith (Smiling)

Everyone leaves the meeting with Keith and go about their own business ...

Keith puts out the "A" board in front of the Locarno ...

It reads as follows ...

BRADFORD MECCA LOCARNO PRESENTS

NEW YEAR'S EVE BALL AND DISCO

A NIGHT OF NON-STOP DANCING

ALL TICKETS – SOLD OUT!!!

LAST REMAINING ENTRY – 50 ONLY ON THE DOOR

8PM - 1AM ... MIDNIGHT COUNTDOWN TO BIG BEN

DJ MARTIN TWIST AND THE BOBBY BROOK BAND

FANCY DRESS OPTIONAL

PARTY CELEBRATION NIGHT

Meanwhile, Mark and Ray have made up with Mary and Mandy.

All four meet prior to the event of the year at Bradford Mecca!

All are wearing fancy dress outfits ...

Mark is the captain out of a Space Television series ... Mandy and Mary are sexy Nurses ... and Ray is a Rockstar!

Somewhere in a popular bar in Bradford City Centre ...

"We had thought about doing the double tonight" advises Ray

"Double?" asks Mandy (Looks intrigued)

"Yea ... the Hole in the Wall, as well" adds Mark (Smiling)

"Is it open?" asks Mary (Looks stunning)

"Naturally, it's New Year's Eve" replies Ray (Smiles)

"Don't you think we're over dressed for that?" asks Mary

"Well, you two aren't that's for sure" laughs Mark

"What do you mean?" asks Mandy (Sounds stunned)

"If you bend over in those skimpy uniforms everyone will see what you had for breakfast" laughs Ray

"Cheeky" replies Mandy (Laughing)

Earlier in the day, the case against married Priest ... Father Shamus Rafferty is unfolding in Bradford's Crown Court.

He is suspected of rape after kissing a girl 16 ...

"These are serious charges ... Mr. Rafferty" advises the Chief Prosecutor (Looks stern)

The jury is out, but suddenly returns to Court.

The Judge presiding asks if they have reached a majority verdict.

The Forman of the Jury stands up ...

"Have you reached a majority decision?" asks the Judge (Looks serious)

"We have, Your Worship" replies the Forman (Looks equally serious)

"Do you find the defendant, Father Shamus Rafferty guilty or not guilty?" asks the Judge

"Guilty" replies the Forman (Gasps from all around the Court)

The Judge, Michael Merryman, QC, addresses the Jury ...

"A lot of thought has been given about the sentence the defendant will receive" advises the Judge (Looks serious)

"This could include an immediate prison term" adds the Judge

"I have an open mind on passing sentence" concludes the Judge

"Rafferty will be sentenced following reports on March 1st" explains the Judge (Looks serious)

It is now almost 8pm at the Bradford Locarno.

Keith and his door staff eagerly await the New Year revelers and are ready to greet them in the Foyer ...

Mark, Ray, Mandy, and Mary arrive in the entrance and Foyer ...

"Superb fancy dress" advises Keith (Smiling)

"You know who we are don't you?" asks Ray (Looks intrigued)

"Naturally, you're among our best customers ... come into my office for a treat" replies Keith (Smiles)

Mark, Ray, Mandy, and Mary all enter Keith's office for a champagne reception and a surprise presentation of "lifetime" passes to the Mecca!

They are all stunned!

"Thank you so much, Keith" advises Mandy (Kisses

Keith on cheek)

"Your all life members of the Locarno ... you can come as often as you like on your free passes" explains Keith

Mark and Ray shake hands with Keith ... while Mary places a smacker on his lips ...

"How long do they last, Keith?" asks Ray (Looks stunned)

"A lifetime" replies Keith (Smiling)

"So, we hope you will stay with us and become part of the family?" advises Keith

"Yes, of course Keith we always feel at home here" replies Mark and Ray

The music in the ballroom is now in full swing ...

DJ Martin is playing a selection of Christmas hits coupled with plenty of party songs!

Suddenly, the stage revolves to the sound of "Time is Tight" and the Bobby Brook Band continues the party atmosphere.

The dance floor is packed with lots of dancers and New Year's Eve revelers ...

Bobby winks at Jackie and she blushes ...

Mark, Ray, Mandy, and Mary take to the dance floor ...

Everyone in the venue is enjoying themselves.

Bobby Brook announces a change over to the popular "Barn dance"

"OK, please take your partners for the Barn dance"

advises Bobby (Smiling)

"We'll sit this one out" advises Ray (Laughs)

"Yea, I need a breather" adds Mark (Looks exhausted)

"OK ... we're going on the floor" advises Mandy (Smiles)

Mary and Mandy take to the dance floor ...

What seems an eternity, the changeover dance ends but there is no sign of Mandy or Mary!

Ray and Mark assume the worst!

"What's happened to those two?" asks Mark (Looks concerned)

"Maybe it was not such a good idea to let them go" adds Mark

Ray spots Mandy and Mary being chatted up by another couple of blokes ...

"Well, the bare faced cheek of it" advises Ray (Looks mad)

"What's happening, Ray?" asks Mark (Looks concerned)

"It looks like Mandy and Mary have been pulled by another two blokes" replies Ray

"It's probably all very harmless" advises Mark (Sounds innocent)

"I don't call being snogged up, harmless" advises Ray (Looks annoyed)

"Not Mary ... she wouldn't do that to me" replies Mark

"Oh, yes she would ... look" explains Ray (Points)

"Your right ... can you believe it?" adds Mark (Looks stunned)

"Well, two can play that game ... come on" advises Ray

"Where are we going?" asks Mark (Looks serious)

"Back on the dance floor ... time for us to make our mark" replies Ray

Mark and Ray head back on to the dance floor and immediately dance with a couple of blondes ...

"Hi ... I'm Ray" advises Ray (Smiling)

"Steph" replies a girl with long blonde hair (Smiles)

"Hi ... I'm Mark" introduces Mark (Smiles)

"Carol" replies the other girl also with long blonde hair (Smiling)

Mandy and Mary are oblivious to everything and don't return to be with Mark and Ray ... they are both preoccupied with the other men!

Meanwhile, Ray and Mark are in seventh heaven with Steph and Carol.

"You're not both Nurses, are you?" asks Ray (Looks concerned)

"No ... we both work in the city, love" advises Steph (Big Smile)

"Why ... wouldn't you danced with us if we had been?" asks Carol

"Yes, of course we would" replies Ray (Smiles)

All four end the night with Auld Lang syne at Midnight with lots of kisses and promises of a date.

Mandy and Mary are nowhere to be seen!

Next day, New Year's Day ... Mark decides to head into Bradford and goes to see Mary at the Nurses Home at Saint Lukes Hospital.

Mark catches up with Mary as she is about to enter the home ...

"Hello Mary" greets Mark (Smiles)

"Oh ... it's you" replies Mary (Looks stunned)

"Well, who else were you expecting?" asks Mark (Looks round)

"I'm sorry but I have to go" advises Mary (Looks serious)

"Thank you for a lovely time" adds Mary

Mark is left speechless on the doorstep!

Mary enters the Nurses Home.

Mark knows that it is all over between him and Mary.

Mark goes home and is given some good advice by his Mum ...

He meets Ray in Bradford later ...

Mark relays his story to Ray.

"Well, I guess that's that" advises Ray

"My Mum gave me some good advice though" advises Mark (Smiles)

"What did she say?" asks Ray (Looks intrigued)

"Always remember, there's as good a fish in the sea that ever came out of it" replies Mark (Smiling)

"Do you know what?" asks Ray

"What?" asks Mark

"Your Mum is right ... spot on" replies Ray (Smiles)

"Come on ... remember we promised to meet Steph and Carol later" advises Ray (Face lights up)

"Yes, I remember" replies Mark

"We also have our lifetime passes for Bradford Mecca" adds Ray

"There's always a cloud with a silver lining" quips Mark (Laughs)

"Come on, let's go back to our old stomping ground" explains Ray (Both Laughing)

"What about Steph and Carol?" asks Mark

"Don't you remember we promised to meet them outside?" replies Ray

THE HOLE IN THE WALL

It's back to 1967 and the Swinging Sixties for this comedy/drama set of stories!

College friends, Richard and Gerry discover coming of age through the magic of Tamla Motown and Soul music at the legendary Continental Coffee Bar in Bradford.

The Hole in the Wall is where all the action takes place ... and it's where everyone wants to be!

It's a time when Mod mania reigns supreme!

Mini skirted girls are everywhere ... but growing up is never easy, especially if you have been brought up in a World of innocence!

The World has changed this is the time of the permissive society and flower power!

Richard and Gerry eventually progress to the Bradford Locarno where more adventures lie ahead ...

THIS IS MY WORLD, TODAY!

THE LEGEND BEGINS

PRESENT DAY ...

Richard and Gerry decide to meet up at the Crowne Plaza Hotel in Leeds within the Bar/Restaurant area.

Both begin to reminisce about their wonderful times back in the Swinging Sixties at the legendary Hole in the Wall!

At a table away from the bar area, both remember the good times back then ...

"Richard ... do you remember all the good times we had at the Continental Coffee Bar in Bradford?" asks Gerry (Looks serious)

"Yes, very much so ... particularly the Hole in the Wall" replies Richard (Smiles)

"I fondly remember all the Tamla Motown and Soul music ... and all the mini skirted girls" adds Gerry (Laughs)

"Yes, I particularly remember them too" adds Richard

(Nods)

"Remember all the girls we met and how many we took out?" asks Gerry (Looks inquisitive)

"Oh yea, I remember ... we were never that good ... too shy" replies Richard (Laughs)

"Your absolutely right of course, Rich ... if only we could go back to those days again, it would be fantastic" advises Gerry (Dreaming)

"I agree ... those were the best times" explains Richard (Smiles)

"Do you remember ... Arthur Conley's Sweet Soul Music?" asks Gerry

"Oh yea ... I can hear it now" replies Richard (Looks happy)

BACK TO MARCH 1967 ...

Saturday Night from 3pm till 9.30pm ... THE HOLE IN THE WALL is full to the brim ...

Richard and Gerry, both teenagers agree to meet outside the Bradford Library Theatre at 7pm ...

Richard arrives and greets Gerry outside the glass doors ...

"You're looking trendy" advises Richard (Smiles)

"Well, I wasn't sure what to wear, Rich" greets Gerry (Smiling)

"I thought this might be appropriate" adds Gerry

Gerry is dressed in a white shirt with black tie, black trousers, and a brown imitation leather jacket!

"You look good too, Rich" replies Gerry (Smiles)

"Is it real leather, Gerry?" asks Richard (Looks serious)

"Yes, of course ... what do you think?" adds Gerry (Laughs)

We start walking down the road towards a hill leading up to the Continental Coffee Bar.

THE HOLE IN THE WALL is situated on the traffic lights opposite Sunwin House.

There is a sign above the door down to the basement ... it shows a mini skirted girl passing a bottle of cola to a boy through a hole in the wall!

Gerry and Richard enter down the stairs into the Coffee Bar area which is to the left of them.

It has lots of tables and chairs with some pinball machines.

Lots of Mods are inside with their Lambretta's parked outside.

THE HOLE IN THE WALL is a skinhead's haunt and there are Parka jackets all over the place ... there seems to be lots of snogging going on with lots of teenage girls!

On the right is the legendary HOLE IN THE WALL ... it's free entry and we're met by Arthur Conley's Sweet Soul Music belting out on the twin deck turntables followed by lots more Soul songs ...

We are now on the floor ... no partners back then ... we all loved the music!

"Come on Rich ... we have to dance to this" advises Gerry (Smiles)

Richard didn't need asking twice ...

Gerry is 13 and Richard is 15 ... both are teenagers and at College in Bradford.

We danced next to several girls dancing together around their handbags.

We were dancing together too ... nobody thought anything of it in those days ... there was nothing to it ...

We were all young and growing up together ... that's the way it was!

The DJ played non-stop Motown and Soul stuff ...

"Hey, look at that fluorescent tube on the ceiling" advises Gerry (Pointing)

It was showing up all the bits on our clothes!

"Is Geoff coming tonight, Rich?" asks Gerry

Geoff is also from college but older than us ... it was very much our World today!

"He said he might come later with Jack" explains Richard (Smiles)

"OK ... we'll watch out for them" replies Gerry (Smiling)

Richard suddenly notices that Geoff is on his way into

the Hole in the Wall ...

"Here he comes" advises Richard (Smiling)

Geoff is about 6 feet tall, very slim, originally from Uganda but recently came to the UK as Idi Amin expelled everyone. Amin was a dictator!

"I've got you two a cola" advises Geoff (Smiling)

"Oh, thanks Geoff ... we'll be there in a jiffy, mate" replies Gerry (Smiles)

"Well, how have you two been getting on with the girls?" asks Geoff

"Oh, fabulous ... just fabulous" replies Gerry (Looks sheepish)

"We've just danced on our own" advises Richard (Laughs)

Geoff also laughs and we all decide to claim our colas ...

"I don't know what to say to them" explains Gerry (Looks shy)

"Just say ... do you come here often?" adds Richard (Smiles)

"Why don't you say it, Rich?" asks Gerry (Looks serious)

"Because I thought you might" replies Richard (Sounds sincere)

The DJ changes over from Motown to Soul and the music is deafening!

Suddenly, one of Geoff's friends walks towards us ...

"Hi Jack, are you OK?" asks Gerry (Smiles)

Jack is about five feet 7, has black hair and sultry looking ...

"Swell ... come on let's get on that floor" replies Jack (Smiling)

So, now there are four of us all dancing together in our group ...

"OK ... you remember to ask if they come here often, Gerry" advises Richard (Smiling)

"Yea, OK, Rich ... I will" replies Gerry (Smiles)

An opportunity suddenly arises ...

Two very slim mini skirted girls, both about 16, one blonde the other brunette dance close to our group ...

"This is your moment, Gerry" advises Richard (Smiles)

"Yes ... go on" adds Geoff (Pushes Gerry close to them)

"OK, I will do it ... but you next alright?" replies Gerry (Looks shy)

"OK, sure" replies Richard (Smiling)

The music is now playing so loud no one can hear what Gerry says!

Both girls smile and carry on dancing ...

"You're in there" advises Geoff (Laughs)

"They like you, Gerry" adds Richard (Smiling)

"Well, what are you going to do next?" asks Geoff (Sounds serious)

"Oh, well ... nothing" replies Gerry (Looks shy)

"Nothing ... what are you doing?" laughs Geoff

"What about you two?" asks Gerry (Pointing)

"Come on Jack we will try our luck" advises Geoff

"Yea ... show us how it's done" adds Gerry (Smiles)

It's a very dark room with rounded ceilings and only has the odd spotlight apart from the fluorescent tubes.

The atmosphere and music are electric!

"OK, I will have another go" advises Gerry (Smiling)

"Jack, are you ready?" asks Gerry (Points)

"OK, Gerry ... let's go" replies Jack (Smiles)

They both look around the floor and decide to ask someone sat down ...

"I will ask that one if you ask the other" explains Gerry

"Yea, OK ... let's do it" replies Jack (Laughs)

Gerry wanders up to the first girl ...

"Excuse me, can I have this dance, love?" asks Gerry (Smiling)

"I'll give you dancing" replies a bloke's voice (Gerry looks stunned)

"I'm sorry ... they put me up to it" replies Gerry (Looks embarrassed)

"OK ... anyone can make a mistake ... but remember next time" advises the bloke (Laughs)

"Yes, I will ... sorry again" replies Gerry (Very apologetic)

Richard, Jack, and Geoff are all laughing ...

"Well, at least you did ask someone to dance, Gerry" laughs Richard

"OK, I get it ... next time it's the real thing" advises Gerry

"Next time?" asks Richard (Looks intrigued)

"Yes ... my confidence is now growing" explains Gerry (Smiling)

BACK TO THE PRESENT DAY ...

"Oh, I remember that ... I was so naive back then" laughs Gerry

"We were all green back then, Gerry" adds Richard (Smiles)

"Do you remember the pinball machines, Rich?" asks Gerry

"Oh yea ... and the time we were at the Mecca and a young blonde summoned us up from the dance floor" adds Richard

"Well?" asks Richard (Looks intrigued)

"That's another story for another day" replies Gerry (Laughs)

"The Bradford Mecca on Manningham Lane was all shiny and new ... I remember it so well" adds Gerry

"Yea but the blonde was a bit tasty" adds Richard

"Can you recall it, Gerry?" asks Richard

"I'll have to think about that one" replies Gerry (Laughs)

TEENAGERS IN THE SWINGING SIXTIES

PRESENT DAY ...

Richard and Gerry continue to reminisce about their good times in the Swinging Sixties.

They continue to chat at the Crowne Plaza and it's not long before they cast their minds back in time ...

"I wonder whatever happened to Geoff and Jack?" asks Gerry (Looks concerned)

"I don't know ... it's as if they just disappeared off the planet" replies Richard

"The last time I saw Geoff he was running a shop close to Saint Lukes Hospital in Bradford ... but that was decades ago" explains Gerry

"Do you remember our first time at Bradford Mecca?" asks Richard

"Oh, yea ... it was all shiny and new then ... I can

still smell the burgers and coffee" advises Gerry (Looks serious)

> *It's 1967 and Richard asks Gerry to accompany him to the Tuesday Teenagers Night at the Mecca Locarno on Manningham Lane in Bradford.*

Richard is 15 and Gerry is 13 ... both attend the same College in Morley Street ...

"Oh, I would love to go" advises Gerry (Looks excited)

"OK ... meet as usual outside the Library Theatre about 7pm" replies Richard

"OK ... I can't wait to go, Rich" replies Gerry (Still excited)

Richard and Gerry arrive at the Mecca Locarno. They have never seen such a big venue with such an enormous dance floor.

The Bobby Brook Band played "Live," and it had a DJ playing up to date pop and Soul music ...

"Oh wow ... this is the place to be, Rich" advises Gerry (Sounds excited)

It's the change over from the Live band to the records section ...

Time is Tight is now playing ...

"Have you been practicing your dancing?" asks Richard (Looks impressed)

"Well, I have sort of copied one or two styles of dance" explains Gerry (Smiles)

"You're having me on?" replies Richard (Laughs)

"No ... let's see if it provokes a response" adds Gerry (Smiling)

The DJ begins to play upbeat pop music coupled with Tamla Motown ...

The dance floor quickly fills up with lots of other teenagers ...

"We'll dance in the middle" advises Richard (Points)

"OK ... then if we pluck up the courage, we'll ask someone" adds Gerry

"You've suddenly become of age" replies Richard (Looks stunned)

"Well, I'm only thirteen but I will have a go, Rich" explains Gerry (Sounds all grown up)

"I'm only fifteen" adds Richard (Laughs)

Gerry and Richard begin to dance next to lots of young girls all dressed in miniskirts ... when suddenly Gerry is tapped on the shoulder ...

"Hi" greets a young brunette (Smiling)

"You see that blonde girl sat down overlooking the balcony?" (She suddenly waves) asks the brunette

(Smiles)

"She would like to meet and talk to you" adds the brunette

Richard and Gerry are stunned but decide to follow instructions ...

"OK ... I will follow you up" replies Gerry (Smiling)

"This seems interesting, Rich" advises Gerry (Looks surprised)

"I wonder what she wants?" asks Richard (Looks stunned)

Gerry and Richard both walk up the flight of stairs to the balcony with the young brunette and approach the stunning blonde ...

"Hi ... I'm Paula" greets the stunning blonde (Big Smile)

"Hi ... I'm Gerry ... this is Richard" greets Gerry (Looks stunned)

"Oh ... I like your dancing" advises Paula (Smiling)
"Well, thanks ... I'm glad someone noticed" replies Gerry (Smiles)

PRESENT DAY ...

"Do you remember what happened next, Rich?" asks Gerry

"No ... remind me?" asks Richard (Looks pensive)

BACK TO 1967 ...

"I just wanted you to know" adds Paula (Smiling)

"Well, OK ... thanks" replies Gerry (Looks embarrassed)

"Drat you were in there ... pity she had someone already in tow" advises Richard (Smiles)

"Let's take it as an omen, Rich" replies Gerry (Laughs)

The records section is now winding down ... Time is Tight is now playing again with the "Live" Bobby Brook Band ...

Bobby makes a sudden announcement ...

"Please take your partners for the barn dance" asks Bobby (Smiling)

"Oh, I can't do that, Rich" advises Gerry

"OK ... I'm going to have a go" explains Richard (Flexes chest)

"And while I'm doing it, I will chat to a few girls and make them aware of us" advises Richard (Smiling)

Richard is gone ages, and now there are lots of young teenagers snogging in the corners of the Mecca ...

Suddenly, Richard returns ...

"Well, how did you get on, Rich?" asks Gerry (Looks serious)

"I had a few little chats but nothing over the top"

advises Richard (Smiles)

"What did you say to them, Rich?" asks Gerry (Looks intrigued)

"Why ... do you come here often of course" explains Richard (Laughs)

"Did it work, Rich?" asks Gerry (Looks serious)

"Well, it got us talking ... we will both try it sometime" adds Richard

PRESENT DAY ...

"Oh ... they were wonderful days" advises Richard (Smiles)

"Yea ... we were so polite, Rich" replies Gerry (Smiling)

"But that's how it was back then" adds Richard

"I remember we had good manners and always cleanly dressed" adds Gerry

"I also remember your Mum asking if you had got a clean handkerchief and saying that you will never get a girl if you didn't look the part" explains Gerry (Smiling)

"Yea, me too" replies Richard (Laughs)

"Our Mum's were always right" adds Gerry (Smiling)

"We were all so innocent back then, but we were really scared to do anything" advises Gerry

"I remember ... we all were back then ... not just us" admits Richard

"Do you remember when we visited Blackpool and the discos we used to go to together, Rich?" asks Gerry

Richard nods and Gerry begins to reminisce ...

> *It's now set in Blackpool circa 1968 at a downstairs discotheque close to Central Pier ...*

Richard and Gerry are on a day trip to the resort!

It's raining cats and dogs in Blackpool!

"The weather's lousy ... why don't we try our hand in here?" asks Gerry

The sign outside the venue indicates "AFTERNOON DISCO in Basement"

"Yea, it sounds like fun" replies Richard (Smiles)

"Well, it beats getting wet in all this rain" adds Gerry

"OK, lead the way" advises Richard (Pointing)

Gerry and Richard proceed down the stairs into the Basement.

As they enter the large area there are already lots of boys and girls on the dance floor ...

PRESENT DAY

"I remember now" explains Richard (Sighs)

"Yea, but do you remember the girls we met there?" asks Gerry

Richard looks puzzled ...

"No, not really ... how did we get on?" asks Richard (Looks inquisitive)

BACK TO BLACKPOOL, 1968 ...

Lots of Soul and Pop songs are being played loudly ...

"Come on, Rich ... let's take a chance with those two over there" advises Gerry (Points)

"You only live once" adds Gerry (Laughs)

Richard and Gerry venture on to the dance floor, and pluck up the courage to talk to the girls already on the floor ...

"Hi, I'm Gerry ... this is Richard" advises Gerry (Smiling)

"Hi, I'm Sue ... this is Anne" replies one of the girls (Big Smile)

As I remember, they were both stunners ...

Sue looked about 16, blonde, petite, dressed in the fashions of the day, and a short miniskirt.

Anne was a striking brunette, also about 16, she was well-spoken and wearing a tight miniskirt.

"Do you come here often?" asks Gerry (Smiles)

"No ... we're both from Cambridge" replies Sue (Big Smile)

"Where are you from?" asks Sue (Looks inquisitive)

"Oh, we're both from Leeds" adds Gerry (Smiling)

"Rich this is Sue" explains Gerry

"Hi, Sue" replies Richard (Smiles)

"Say Hi to Anne, Gerry" adds Richard

"Hi, Anne" replies Gerry (Smiling)

"Are you both here on holiday?" asks Gerry (Smiles)

"Yes, we're here for a week" replies Sue (Smiles)

"What about you?" asks Sue (Big Smile)

"Oh, no ... it's just a day out for us" replies Gerry

"Oh, that's a pity" adds Anne (Sighs)

"We might go for a walk on the beach later ... do you fancy joining us?" asks Sue (Smiles)

"Yea, why not?" replies Richard (Looks excited)

"What time do you have to leave?" asks Anne

"Oh, we're booked on the 7.30pm train from Blackpool North to Leeds" advises Richard (Looks at watch)

"Oh, there's plenty of time then" replies Sue (Smiling)

"Plenty of time for what?" asks Gerry (Looks puzzled)

"Come on let's go for a walk" replies Sue (Winks)

Gerry and Richard both walk hand in hand with Sue

and Anne ...

There is plenty of snogging and cuddling along the way.

All four walk out of the venue and are now facing Central Pier ...

"Fancy a walk on the pier?" asks Richard (Smiles)

"Yea, why not" replies Anne (Smiling)

"What about under the pier for a quick snog?" adds Anne

Gerry and Richard both look gob smacked!

"Sorry love we can't the tides in" advises Gerry (Looks miffed)

"Tell you what ... why don't we all go to the Pleasure Beach ... the tunnel of Love" advises Sue (Looks mischievous)

"You're a fast worker ... OK, let's go for it" replies Gerry

PRESENT DAY

"Do you remember the tunnel of love, Rich?" asks Gerry

"Vaguely ... go on tell me more" replies Richard (Looks inquisitive)

BACK TO THE PLEASURE

BEACH, 1968 ...

Sue, Anne, Richard, and Gerry arrive outside the Tunnel of Love ... and take separate boats ...

"Hey, who turned the lights out?" asks Gerry (Laughs)

Sue moves in for a kiss and a cuddle ...

Suddenly, the ride halts!

A voice shouts through the tunnel ...

"Is everyone OK in there?" asks the voice (Sounds concerned)

"Yea, what's going on?" asks Richard (Sounds serious)

"We'll have you out in a jiffy ... an electrical breakdown" advises the voice

"We might as well have another kiss" advises Sue

"Yea, why not?" replies Gerry (Moves in)

"Rich ... are you and Anne, OK?" shouts Gerry (Sounds concerned)

"Oh, yes ... I have got my hands full here" laughs Richard

The ride, eventually, starts to move again ... everyone gets out of the tunnel safely ...

Richard looks at his watch ...

"Sorry, girls ... we have to go" advises Richard (Looks serious)

"It's been a fantastic day ... we will never forget you"

adds Gerry

"If you are ever in Cambridge look us up" replies Sue (Smiling)

"Likewise, if you're both in Leeds" advises Richard

All four exchange telephone numbers and addresses. They all vow to keep in touch ...

PRESENT DAY

"What happened then?" asks Richard (Looks serious)

"We never saw them again ... but what a day" replies Gerry (Smiling)

That is what it was like to be a teenager in the Swinging Sixties!

THAT'S ONE SMALL STEP FOR MAN, ONE GIANT LEAP FOR ME!

PRESENT DAY

Gerry and Richard fondly remember 1969 and the NASA Man on the Moon landings!

There are more visits to the legendary HOLE IN THE WALL, and the BRADFORD MECCA LOCARNO BALLROOM ...

"1969 was an amazing year ... and it's now over 50 years ago" advises Gerry (Looks to be in dreamland)

"Do you remember what happened then, Rich?" adds Gerry

"Oh, yea the Moon Landings ... and we were getting more and more daring too" replies Richard (Smiles)

"Yea, but there were problems at the Hole in the Wall"

advises Gerry

"Oh, I remember the faceoff between the Mods and the Rockers" replies Richard

"That's it ... luckily we didn't get caught up in that" explains Gerry

BACK TO JUNE 1969 ... before the Moon Landings ...

The music was changing ... there seemed to be more bubblegum pop in the charts, but it was as good as ever!

"It'll be number one next week" advises Richard (Looks philosophical)

"Yea, I think your right, Rich" replies Gerry (Smiles)

"What about another visit to the Mecca on Friday night?" asks Richard

Gerry and Richard are in conversation at college ...

"You can stay at mine, if you want to" advises Geoff (Smiling)

"OK, I'll ask my Mum and Dad if it's OK" replies Gerry (Looks excited)

"Did you hear that French song on the radio?" asks Richard

"Which song?" asks Gerry (Looks puzzled)

"It's called Jetaime" replies Richard (Smiles)

"I've never heard of it ... is it a groover?" asks Gerry (Looks stunned)

"No, it's a smooch song" advises Richard (Laughs)

"Well, if I do hear it, I will let you know, Rich" replies Gerry

"It won't be on again ... the BBC have just banned it" replies Geoff

"That's a sure way of making it a number one hit ... everyone will buy it now" adds Richard (Laughs)

"So, what shall we do tonight?" asks Gerry (Looks intrigued)

"What about going to the Hole in the Wall?" asks Richard

"Well, I'm up for it on Saturday ... if you are, Rich" replies Gerry (Smiling)

Richard, Gerry, and Geoff are all in agreement ...

Friday night arrives and Richard and Gerry meet as arranged near the Bradford Library Theatre with Geoff and Jack this time!

Geoff is wearing a stylish red jacket ...

"I like your jacket, Geoff ... it looks very trendy" advises Gerry (Smiles)

The jacket is a vivid red zip up ...

"It should attract the girls" replies Geoff (Laughs)

Richard, Gerry, Geoff, and Jack arrive at the Mecca Locarno on Manningham Lane in Bradford ... they all pay their entry fees and walk into the STAG ROOM ...

"Stop looking at yourself in all those mirrors" laughs Geoff

"I want to make sure my hair is OK, and I look good" replies Gerry

"Take me as I am" adds Jack (All Laugh)

"Yea, me too" advises Richard (Now also laughing)

All four enter the Ballroom and lots of Sixties pop songs are ringing out ...

They all decide to go on the dance floor ...

"OK, remember don't come off the dance floor if you get rejected" advises Geoff (Smiles)

"Well, what if we do?" asks Gerry (Looks intrigued)

"Just go to the next two, and so on ... until your matched up" adds Geoff (Laughs)

"OK, now I understand" replies Gerry (Laughs)

The music changes to Tamla and Soul ...

"OK, come on let's take a chance" advises Richard

"Don't forget to ask them ... do you come here often?" adds Richard

"OK, I won't, Rich" replies Gerry (Smiles)

Richard and Gerry ask a couple of blondes in miniskirts ... but there is no response!

Gerry and Richard move across to the next couple of girls ...

They ask a young blonde and a red head ... they say OK!

Both girls look about 15, slim, cute, and attractive.

"Hi ... I am Gerry ... this is Rich" greets Gerry (Smiling)

"Hi, I'm Mandy ... that's Linda" replies Mandy (Big Smile)

"Do you both come here often?" asks Richard (Smiles)

"Hey, you've just stolen my line" replies Gerry (Laughs)

Both girls are laughing ...

"You two have done it before haven't you?" asks Linda (Smiling)

"No, we haven't you're both in a select few" explains Gerry

"What about you, Gerry?" asks Mandy (Smiles)

"Oh, I'm very experienced ... not" replies Gerry (Laughs)

The DJ changes to more upbeat pop songs ...

"Oh, we love this" advises Mandy (Smiling)

"Stay with us, love" adds Mandy (Winks)

The music suddenly changes to Time is Tight, the records section and the stage revolves to reveal the Bobby Brook Band playing live.

Mandy and Linda continue to groove on the large dance floor which is now full of revelers.

Richard leaves the dance floor and finds a table close to

the bar ...

"I will just see if Richard is OK" advises Gerry (Smiles)

"See you later, Mandy" adds Gerry (Winks)

"Yes, we'll dance again, love" replies Mandy (Smiling)

Gerry leaves the dance floor and heads over to the table where Richard is now sitting ...

"Are you, OK, mate?" asks Gerry (Looks concerned)

"Oh, yea ... it was getting hot out there ... how did you get on?" asks Richard (Looks inquisitive)

"Yea, Mandy is a nice girl ... if nothing else happens tonight I'm a happy boy" advises Gerry (Smiles)

"We have lift off" replies Richard (Smiling)

"Hey, it's the Apollo Moon landing tomorrow" adds Gerry

Suddenly, Time is Tight is being played and the records section returns ...

The DJ starts to play several upbeat Soul records ...

"Hey, we know that DJ" advises Richard

"Who is he, Rich?" asks Gerry (Looks serious)

"He spins the discs at the Hole in the Wall" explains Richard

"He will probably be spinning them tomorrow" adds Richard

We see Mandy and Linda again, but both are now dancing with someone else!

"Oh, don't worry about that" advises Richard (Smiles)

"It was good while it lasted, Rich" replies Gerry (Looks sad)

"There's plenty more fish in the sea" quips Richard (Laughs)

We were on cloud nine ... both young teenagers enjoying the moment!

PRESENT DAY

"I remember it well, Rich" advises Gerry

"It was so innocent back then" adds Gerry (Smiling)

"Yes, I agree it really was" replies Richard (Smiles)

"If we had a dance with a girl or a snog it made our night" explains Gerry (Laughs)

"Those were very special times" adds Gerry

"Very special indeed" replies Richard

"Hey, what happened to Geoff and Jack that night?" asks Richard

BACK TO JULY 1969

"Hi, Geoff ... how is it going?" asks Richard (Looks inquisitive)

"Oh, we've been dancing with two birds ... how about you?" asks Geoff

"So have we ... it's been a fantastic night" replies Gerry (Smiling)

"Seeing as you are stopping at my place ... we will stay until the end" explains Geoff

The dance was from 8pm till 1am in those days!

"OK, fine by me ... what about you, Rich?" asks Gerry

"We might as well make the most of it, Gerry" replies Richard

The DJ makes an announcement ...

"OK, it's time for a smooch" advises the DJ (Smooching sounds)

"Oh, this will be interesting" replies Richard (Smiling)

Mandy and Linda suddenly return ...

"OK, you two ... you didn't think we wouldn't come back, did you?" asks Linda (Big Smile)

"Er ... No ... well" replies a stunned Richard and Gerry (Smiling)

"Come on, you two ... time for a smooch" advises Mandy (Smiles)

So, there they were ... Richard 15 and Gerry 13 ... this was going to be interesting!

Mandy, Linda, Richard, and Gerry all walk towards the dance floor.

The lights are dimmed giving it an intimate atmosphere ...

"Put your arms around me and keep close" advises

Mandy (Smiling)

"You haven't done this before have you, Gerry?" asks Mandy

"No, first time, Mandy" replies Gerry (Looks shy)

"Well, I had better make it a first time to remember then" explains Mandy (Smiling)

"Time for a snog" adds Mandy (Kissing)

PRESENT DAY

It was all very innocent, yet that first kiss is the one you always remember ...

"I wonder what happened to Mandy?" asks Gerry (Looks thoughtful)

"Or Linda for that matter" replies Richard (Tries to remember)

They were all fabulous innocent days ...

"Mandy and Linda are part of that magical time, Rich ... just as we are" advises Gerry (Smiling)

"We lived through it all" replies Richard (Smiles)

"There really will never be a time like the Swinging Sixties again" explains Gerry

"You can say that again, mate" adds Richard

SOUL FINGER

Richard and Gerry continue their conversations at the Crowne Plaza Hotel in Leeds with regards THE HOLE IN THE WALL!

"Hey, Rich ... do you remember SOUL FINGER?" asks Gerry

"It was always a favourite at The Hole in the Wall" adds Gerry (Smiles)

"No ... you'll have to remind me" replies Richard (Looks inquisitive)

LATE 1970 ...

Another Saturday night at the legendary Soul Club ...

Lots of great Soul music is now being played by the regular DJ ...

"Here we are ... another great night" advises Gerry (Smiling)

"Shall we dance with these two?" asks Gerry (Points)

"Yea, why not ... let's go for it" replies Richard (Looks serious)

"What have we got to lose?" asks Gerry (Looks concerned)

"Everything" laughs Richard

"Nothing ventured" replies Gerry (Smiling)

"Nothing gained" adds Richard (Now also Smiling)

Gerry and Richard go on to the packed dance floor ...

"May we have this dance?" asks Gerry (Smiles)

"Yes, OK" reply two girls (Big Smile)

"We're in here, Rich" whispers Gerry

The DJ plays Tamla Motown loud ...

"Oh, I love this Sally" advises one of the girls

"Hi I'm Karen ... she's Sally" advises Karen (Smiling)

"Hi I'm Richard ... that's Gerry" replies Richard (Smiles)

Karen is 5ft 4, has chestnut brown hair and green eyes ...

Sally has long blonde hair, blue eyes and both are very slim ... both look 16

"Do you come here often?" asks Gerry (Smiling)

"Oh, how corny ... I bet you say that to all the girls?" laughs Sally

"Well, maybe once or twice" replies Gerry (Laughs)

"Oh, heck you do" laughs Sally

"I like your outfit" advises Sally (Smiling)

"Oh, this is the latest gear, Sally" replies Gerry (Smiles)

"Do you like my miniskirt?" asks Sally (Smiles)

"Oh, I dig your miniskirt love" adds Gez (Winks)

The DJ changes the music to classic Motown ...

"You're a smooth talker" replies Sally (Laughs)

"Hey, where did you learn those dance steps?" asks Sally

"Oh, I copied some of the top of the pops dancers" replies Gerry (Smiles)

"Well, you've learned them to perfection" adds Sally (Claps)

"What do you think of the music, Gerry?" asks Sally (Smiling)

"Oh, it's fab" replies Gerry (Laughs)

"Thunderbirds are go" adds Gerry (Smiles)

"Are we your birds?" asks Karen (Richard looks surprised)

"You could be ... if you want to be" replies Gerry (Looks suspicious)

"Will you buy us a cola?" asks Sally (Smiles)

"We come as a pair, baby" replies Gerry (Laughs)

"Rich ... we're off to get a cola" explains Gerry (Winks)

"Hang on ... I'm coming with Karen" replies Richard (Nods)

"We will have to make tracks soon" advises Karen

(Looks sad)

"Yes, so will we ... we'll walk you to your bus" advises Gerry

"OK ... we will reward you Gerry" advises Sally (Big Smile)

Richard and Gerry accompany Karen and Sally to their bus stop in Bradford City Centre ... all four have a good old snog!

"That's made my night, Rich" advises Gerry (Looks to be on Cloud nine)

"Yea, mine too" replies Richard (Looks in dreamland)

"Casanova ... eat your heart out" adds Gerry (Laughs)

PRESENT DAY

"What a night that was, Rich" advises Gerry (Smiles)

"I'm amazed how you can remember it all ... 50 years on" replies Richard (Looks surprised)

"Oh, all the good memories stay with you" adds Gerry

"Well, you've whetted my appetite ... what happened after that?" asks Richard (Looks puzzled)

"I think we met up with Karen and Sally a few times at the Hole in the Wall" explains Gerry (Looks happy)

"Everyone knew us there" adds Gerry (Smiles)

"I bet they never forgot you and your moves from top of the pops" laughs Richard

"That's for sure" laughs Gerry

Then there was another time ...

"Do you remember the college dance?" asks Gerry (Ponders)

"You'll have to remind me, Gerry" replies Richard

"Well, if you remember back in 1967, they used to have it at the Polish Club in Claremont?" advises Gerry (Smiles)

"Oh, I remember that" advises Richard (Laughs)

"Yea, but do you remember, Lorraine?" asks Gerry (Smiles)

"I think so" replies Richard (Smiling)

BACK TO 1967 ...

It's the night of the school dance and everyone must be on their best behaviour ... when suddenly a problem arises!

Someone brought a couple of rough types with them, and it caused chaos!

Gerry and Richard are decked out in their Sixties gear ...

"Oh, don't mind them, Gerry" advises Richard (Smiling)

"I know ... it's our night" replies Gerry (Smiles)

Suddenly a familiar voice enters the scene ...

"Well, are you going to dance with me or what?" asks the voice

"Maxine" replies a stunned Gerry (Smiling)

Maxine is five foot seven, has shoulder length brown hair, green eyes and attractive. She is 16

"Are you coming, Rich?" asks Gerry (Points to dance floor)

"No, it's just you and me" advises Maxine (Smiling)

"OK, Maxine" replies Gerry (Looks shy)

"What about Rich?" asks Gerry

"He's got his eye on Lorraine ... can you fix it up?" asks Gerry

Richard really looks embarrassed ...

"OK, I will see what I can do" replies Maxine (Winks)

The following Tuesday, Richard and Gerry are back at College talking about the Mecca Locarno in Manningham Lane ... it's the Teenager's Night ...

Richard and Gerry are talking at college ...

"What if I fix you up with a blind date ... are you in?" asks Richard

"OK, why not ... it sounds like fun, Rich" replies Gerry (Smiles)

"Is she pretty ... is she beautiful?" asks Gerry (Sounds inquisitive)

"Oh ... she is really all of that" replies Richard (Smirking)

"OK ... I can't wait" advises Gerry (Smiles)

Richard and Gerry arrive at the Mecca Locarno ...

"Oh, this is my cousin, Amy" advises Richard (Smiles)

"Blow me down ... she is a really big girl" mutters Gerry

"Hi, Gerry" replies Amy (Smiling)

"Hi" adds Gerry (Looks daggers at Richard)

Gerry's face must have given it all away!

"Sorry, Rich ... I must go I'm not feeling very well ... I will see you tomorrow at college" advises Gerry (Looks mad)

PRESENT DAY

"I bet you don't remember that do you, Rich?" asks Gerry (Smiling)

"No, not really ... go on what happened after that?" asks Richard

BACK TO 1967 ...

Next day at College ...

"Thanks Rich ... please don't fix any more blind dates for me, OK?" advises Gerry

"Why?" asks Richard (Looks inquisitive)

"Sorry ... she's just not my type" replies Gerry (Laughs)

"I might as well stay a confirmed bachelor" adds Gerry

That weekend, Richard and Gerry returned to the Hole in the Wall with a few college friends with them ...

"So, this is where you both hang out?" asks Maxine (Smiles)

"Yep ... this is the place" replies Gerry (Smiling)

"Oh, the music is electric ... Tamla Motown and Soul" adds Richard

The DJ ramps up the music and the dance floor fills up in the basement ...

"What do you think, Maxine?" asks Gerry (Smiles)

"Oh, I love it ... I'm glad I came" replies Maxine

"Me, too" replies Lorraine (Smiling)

Maxine and Lorraine are both wearing short miniskirts with white blouses ...

"I wish we had come here before" advises Maxine (Smiling)

"You can always come with us" replies Richard (Smiles)

"As your girlfriends?" asks Maxine (Winks)

"As mates ... if you want to" replies Gerry (Looks shy)

"What do you mean?" asks Maxine (Looks puzzled)

"Nothing really ... we're just all growing up together" adds Richard

"Do you fancy a cola, Maxine?" asks Gerry (Smiling)

"I fancy a snog" replies Maxine (Laughs)

"OK, later" replies Gerry (Winks)

"What about you Lorraine?" asks Richard

"Yea, me too" replies Lorraine (Winks)

The DJ continues to play loud music then begins to tone it down ...

"This is like a smooch" advises Maxine (Drags Gerry on to floor)

"Is it?" asks Gerry (Looks shy)

"Have you ever had a girlfriend before?" asks Maxine (Looks serious)

"Well ... er, no, not really" replies Gerry (Looks sheepish)

All the girls dancing are wearing Sixties mod minidresses or miniskirts ... it was an eye-popping time!

"Well, go on ... what happened after that?" asks Richard (Looks intrigued)

"I'll have to recall that for next time, Rich" replies Gerry

GIMME ... GIMME ... GOOD LOVIN'

Richard and Gerry meet again at the Crowne Plaza Hotel in Leeds and continue to recall their fond memories ...

BACK TO THE SWINGING SIXTIES ...

The Bradford Mecca Locarno ...

It is yet another Friday night ... Richard, Geoff, Jack, and Gerry hear lots of new records belting out ...

"Oh, I like this one" advises Gerry (Smiles)

"It sounds like a number one for sure" replies Richard

"OK, it's time to get on the dance floor" adds Geoff (Smiling)

"Are you ready, Gerry?" asks Geoff (Points)

"Yea ... sure" replies Gerry (Laughs)

"He's all loved up with Maxine at college" reveals Geoff (Smiles)

Gerry looks embarrassed ...

"Are you?" asks Geoff (Looks inquisitive)

"Only in my mind" adds Gerry (Smiles)

"How does she feel?" adds Geoff (Looks surprised)

"I've got no idea" laughs Gerry

"No idea?" replies Geoff (Laughing)

"Don't you think you should find out?" adds Geoff (Looks serious)

"Oh, no ... I don't think I could cope with rejection" replies Gerry (Looks concerned)

"She won't reject you ... she likes you" adds Richard (Smiling)

"I like her too ... but" replies Gerry (Smiles)

"Let's just see how it goes ... OK?" adds Gerry

"You might meet someone here tonight" advises Geoff (Smiling)

"What would you do if you did?" asks Jack (Smiles)

"He would run a mile" laughs Richard

Suddenly, another voice enters the conversation ...

"Fancy meeting you two here tonight" greets the voice

"Why it's Mandy and Linda" advises Steve (Smiling)

"What you all know each other?" asks Geoff (Looks gob smacked)

"Yes, as a matter of fact, we do" replies Gerry (Smiles)

"We were just wondering how you were going on" adds Gerry (Smiling)

"I bet you say that to all the girls" advises Mandy (Winks)

"Only to the one's we like" explains Gerry (Laughs)

"Flatterer" replies Linda (Smiles)

The DJ is now playing upbeat Sixties pop songs ...

"Well, are you going to ask us to dance or what?" asks Linda

"Er, yes ... come on Gerry" advises Richard (Smiling)

PRESENT DAY

"That was a magical moment in time" advises Gerry

"What happened next?" asks Richard (Looks serious)

BACK TO 1969 ...

Richard and Gerry are talking to Mandy and Linda prior to going on the dance floor ...

Geoff and Jack are already on the dance floor with two stunners!

"Do you girls go to the Hole in the Wall?" asks Gerry (Smiles)

"Yes, we've been a couple of times" replies Mandy

EVERLASTING LOVE

(Smiling)

"Why ... are you both asking us out?" asks Linda (Laughs)

"Oh, yea ... it will be a fun night" replies Gerry

"OK ... it's a date, love" advises Mandy (Kisses Gerry on lips)

"A double date with me and Linda" adds Mandy

"Rich ... are you OK with it?" asks Gerry (Winks)

"Oh, sure ... let's go for it" replies Richard (Smiling)

Geoff and Jack arrive back after being on the dance floor and are amazed at Richard and Gerry's luck ...

"You want to watch those two, girls" advises Geoff (Smiling)

"Why, love?" asks Mandy (Smiles)

"Oh ... they are both good catches" adds Jack (Laughs)

"We know when we're on to a good thing" replies Linda

"Shall we go for a cola?" asks Richard (Smiling)

The DJ changes the tempo to Soul and lots of people are now on the dance floor ...

Linda, Richard, and Mandy go on the dance floor ...

"I will catch you all later ... I'm just having a word with Geoff" explains Gerry (Kisses Mandy)

"OK ... don't be long, love" replies Mandy (Smiling)

"Hey, you're in there Gezza" advises Geoff (Laughs)

"Yea, I think you could be right, Geoff" adds Gerry

"Just don't blow it ... OK?" advises Geoff (Looks serious)

"OK, mate ... I won't" replies Gerry

"We will meet later ... you can stay at mine ... or at theirs if you get the invite" adds Geoff (Grins)

"I'm only 15" adds Gerry (Looks stunned)

"It's just a joke, mate" laughs Geoff

"OK" replies Gerry (Laughing)

"Just enjoy yourself" explains Geoff (Winks)

"OK... see you later, Geoff" adds Gerry (Smiles)

The dance floor is almost full ...

Gerry joins Mandy, Linda, and Richard on the floor ...

"What did Geoff want?" asks Richard (Looks intrigued)

"Oh ... he just gave me a little man to man advice" explains Gerry

"Do you like my outfit?" asks Mandy (Smiles)

Mandy is dressed in a short miniskirt with a white blouse ...

"I think it's great, love" replies Gerry (Laughs)

"I'm a student at the University" advises Mandy (Smiling)

"Oh, I'm still at college with Richard" explains Gerry (Smiles)

"What about you Linda?" asks Richard (Looks inquisitive)

"Oh, I'm a trainee hairdresser, love" advises Linda (Smiling)

"What do you want to do when you leave college?" asks Mandy (Smiles)

"Oh, I don't know ... maybe a brain surgeon" quips Gerry (Laughs)

"What about you, Richard?" asks Linda (Looks puzzled)

"Ditto" replies Richard (All Laughing)

Gerry, Mandy, Linda, and Richard remain on the dance floor as the DJ now changes the mood to a party type of atmosphere ...

"Oh, we love this" advises Mandy (Laughs)

"OK, let's stay on the dance floor girls" replies Gerry (Winks)

"You're getting pretty confident" advises Richard

"You know what ... so are you, mate" adds Gerry

"It must be the time and the place" explains Richard

"It won't last forever, Rich" replies Gerry (Looks sad)

"Now is the time of our lives" advises Richard (Smiles)

What more could Richard and Gerry ask for?

This was the place to be ... fantastic music ... with two wonderful girls!

"Just don't grow up so fast, OK?" advises Richard (Smiles)

"Yes, let's just enjoy it while we can, Rich" replies Gerry (Both Laugh)

It's getting to the end of the night ...

Richard and Gerry meet up with Geoff and Jack near the clock at the end of the ballroom ...

"Have you both enjoyed yourselves tonight?" asks Geoff (Looks inquisitive)

"Oh, fabulous time, mate" replies Gerry (Smiles)

"We've arranged a second date with Mandy and Linda at the Hole in the Wall next Saturday" advises Richard (Looks happy)

"How did you and Jack do?" asks Gerry (Looks inquisitive)

"Oh, we've managed to find two girls, too" advises Geoff (Looks pleased)

"Maybe we can have a double date next weekend?" asks Richard

"Maybe" replies Geoff (Smiles)

"What will Maxine think on Monday?" asks Geoff (Sounds serious)

"Maxine?" replies Gerry (Looks stunned)

"She might be jealous" adds Geoff

"Maxine is not my property or date" explains Gerry (Looks serious)

"Are you going to tell her about your catch?" asks Jack

"My catch?" replies Gerry (Looks embarrassed)

"Your allowed to boast, Gerry" explains Geoff (Laughs)

"Yea and I might end up in the doghouse, too" advises Gerry

"Well, she does like you, after all" replies Richard

"Your all talking nonsense" quips Gerry (Laughs)

PRESENT DAY

"Well, what happened then?" asks Richard (Looks intrigued)

"Oh, Geoff was right ... Maxine was not happy" replies Gerry

BACK TO 1969 ...

Monday morning arrives ... Richard and Gerry see Maxine before lessons at college ...

"Did you have a lovely weekend?" asks Maxine (Smiling)

"Well, he did ... especially as he found himself a date" replies Richard (Looks mischievous)

"Thanks, mate ... I'll do the same for you some time" replies Gerry (Looks serious)

"Well, what's she like ... where does she come from?"

asks Maxine (Sounds serious)

"Oh, so and so" advises Gerry (Looks sheepish)

"And I thought I was your number one girl" adds Maxine (Looks sad)

"You are, Maxine ... there is no one like you" replies Gerry

"You will tell me anything ... anyway you know where I am" adds Maxine (Storms off)

"I think you've upset her" advises Richard

"I think I have" replies Gerry (Looks embarrassed)

"What can I do to make it up to her?" asks Gerry

"Nothing ... just play it cool" replies Richard

"It's all part of the game ... Maxine knows the score" adds Richard

"Well, if she didn't ... she does now" quips Gerry

Will Maxine forgive Gerry or has their friendship been ruined because of the differences between them?

SWEET SOUL MUSIC

PRESENT DAY

Richard and Gerry continue their conversations in a trip down memory lane at the Crowne Plaza Hotel in Leeds ...

"Well, what happened when we had our double date at the Hole in the Wall?" asks Richard (Looks inquisitive)

BACK TO 1969 ...

The DJ is playing lots of Soul instrumentals and Tamla Motown at the famous venue.

Richard and Gerry meet outside the Bradford Library Theatre on Saturday at 7pm as arranged.

They make their way to the legendary Continental Coffee Bar.

They meet Mandy and Linda close to the entrance.

All go down the flight of stairs into the basement.

THE HOLE IN THE WALL is to the right of them ...

The DJ is playing all the popular hits, and they are being played loud continually on the on the twin decks which is situated overlooking the dance floor. The speakers are pumping and booming ... music is ringing in your ears!

"Oh, we love these songs" advises Linda (Smiling)

Richard, Linda, Gerry, and Mandy venture on to the now packed dance floor ... the ceiling is curved, and the atmosphere is dimly lit except for the fluorescent lights above them ...

Sly and the Family Stone ... Dance to the Music is playing (Loud)

"Ok ... let's dance to this" replies Richard (Smiling)

All rush on to the dance floor.

It's a wonderful night, and Linda and Mandy are both lovely girls!

"It's getting a bit hot in here ... let's have a cola" advises Richard (Moves towards bar)

"Good idea, Rich" replies Gerry (Smiles)

"OK, girls ... you wait here ... we will be back in a jiffy with the colas" explains Richard

The DJ begins to play various Tamla hits loud ...

"The DJ is on fire tonight, Rich" advises Gerry (Smiling)

"Yes, I agree he has played some great stuff tonight"

replies Richard

The cola drinks are handed to Richard and Gerry ...

"Where are the girls?" asks Richard (Looks baffled)

"Looks like some other blokes have taken them on to the dance floor" replies Gerry

"Well, they are not our property, mate" replies Richard (Sounds logical)

"OK, let's take a breather ... maybe they will join us later" adds Gerry

As Gerry and Richard begin to drink their colas ... a couple of girls come to join them ... and they are both pretty young things too!

"Can we join you?" asks a voice (Smiles)

"Sure, please do" replies Richard (Smiles)

"I'm Sam ... she is Ronnie" advises Sam (Smiling)

Sam is a lovely brunette with brown eyes ... Ronnie is a tall blonde with long legs ... both are similar ages ... about 15 years old

"Oh, I'm Gerry ... and this is Richard" (Smiles)

"Do you come here often?" asks Richard

"We've been a few times ... never seen you two though" replies Ronnie (Smiling)

"Oh, we sometimes go to the Mecca on Manningham Lane ... it's a good night" advises Gerry (Smiling)

"You're both right ... we've been a few times" adds Sam

"We're both going to a party later ... do you want to join us?" asks Sam (Big Smile)

"Well, that's nice of you to ask but we're waiting for someone" explains Richard (Smiles)

"Well, if you both change your mind, we'll be on the dance floor" replies Ronnie (Smiling)

The girls leave and join everyone else on the dance floor ...

"What do you make of that, Rich?" asks Gerry (Looks baffled)

"It seems too good to be true to me" replies Richard (Looks sceptical)

"It might be genuine ... but it may not be" adds Richard

"OK, let's see what happens later" replies Gerry (Looks serious)

"It looks like we're back to how we were for now" explains Richard

"There's no harm in that" adds Gerry (Laughs)

Suddenly, a tap on the shoulder ...

Maxine and Lorraine from college have arrived ...

"Fancy meeting you two here" advises Maxine (Smiling)

"Yep ... you've taken us by surprise" replies Gerry (Smiles)

"Well, are we dancing or what?" asks Maxine (Winks)

The DJ is playing a mix of Soul and Tamla ...

"Sure, Maxine let's dance" replies Gerry (Laughs)

"I thought you might have been spoken for by now" adds Maxine

"You are my only girl, Maxine ... you know that" replies Gerry (Smiles)

"You'll tell me anything" replies Maxine (Laughs)

"Well ... there is something between us that's for sure" advises Gerry

"Oh ... I didn't mean" adds Gerry (Looks shy)

"I know what you meant" replies Maxine (Smiles)

A sudden wave on the dance floor from Mandy ...

"And I suppose she is one of your girls too?" asks Maxine (Looks daggers)

"She's not like you, Maxine" replies Gerry (Looks shy)

"Am I your special girl?" asks Maxine (Winks)

"You could be ... if you wanted to be" advises Gerry

"Smooth talker" laughs Maxine (Kisses on cheek)

PRESENT DAY

"Well, did you take Maxine out or what?" asks Richard (Looks intrigued)

All will be revealed ...

BACK TO 1969 ...

Mandy came back to join us ...

"This is Maxine ... we're close college friends" advises Gerry (Smiles)

"Yea ... very close" adds Maxine (Puts arm round Gerry)

"Yea, I can see that" replies Mandy (Looks stunned)

"Well, I thought" adds Gerry (Looks serious)

"That I wasn't coming back ... right?" asks Mandy (Looks serious)

"Got it in one ... we both did to tell you the truth" replies Richard

"Sorry ... but yes we did think that Mandy" adds Gerry (Looks concerned)

"Well, I hope you two will be very happy" adds Mandy

"We will, love ... thanks" replies Maxine (Puts arm around Gerry)

"What have you done, Maxine?" asks Lorraine (Looks puzzled)

"I'd say that I have saved you from a natural disaster" laughs Maxine

"A natural disaster?" asks Richard (Looks intrigued)

"In what way?" asks Gerry (Looks stunned)

"Yea ... and she was one" quips Maxine (Smiling)

Richard and Gerry both looked stunned at what's just happened ...

"Come on, Maxine ... let's dance" advises Gerry (Smiles)

The DJ changes the music from the up tempo beat to a smooch ...

"You're not going to leave me now, are you?" asks Maxine (Looks serious)

"No, of course not" replies Gerry (Smiles)

"What will they say at college?" asks Gerry (Looks concerned)

"Oh, they already know that I like you" explains Maxine (Big Smile)

"I'm still very young, Maxine" replies Gerry (Looks shy)

"I know ... we are all growing up together" advises Maxine

"Are we more than friends?" asks Maxine (Smiling)

"I would say we are friends for life, Maxine" replies Gerry (Smooching)

"You, me, Lorraine, and Richard ... we're all soul partners" explains Gerry

The DJ changes the mood back up to a Swinging Sixties mix of records ...

"Well, your love just walked away" replies Richard

"Not necessarily" advises Maxine (Smiling)

The DJ plays another hit ... It takes two ...

"Me and you, baby" advises Gerry (Smiles)

"Me and you" replies Maxine (Both start kissing)

The DJ now plays the old Mary Wells hit ... My Guy ...

"See I told you" explains Maxine (Laughs)

"Did you request this?" asks Maxine (Looks suspicious)

"You'll never know, Maxine" replies Gerry

It's coming to the end of the night ... and time for one last dance!

The DJ is now playing Len Barry's hit ... One Two Three ...

"Come on, Maxine, we have just got time for one last boogie" advises Gerry (Smiling)

"You know we will be the talk of the college on Monday" replies Maxine

"I don't care, Maxine ... do you?" asks Gerry (Both smiling)

"No, Gerry ... we have something special" adds Maxine

PRESENT DAY

"I wonder whatever happened to Maxine?" asks Richard (Looks serious)

"I guess we will never know now ... it's over 50 years later, but you never know ... you just never know" replies Gerry

"I've read about a rebirth of THE HOLE IN THE WALL

on the Internet in the next few weeks" advises Gerry (Smiles)

"Do you fancy going, Rich?" asks Gerry

"No, not really" replies Richard (Looks serious)

"Why not?" asks Gerry (Looks puzzled)

"It just won't be the same 50 years on" adds Richard (Looks serious)

"We have all our wonderful memories of the Swinging Sixties and anything else would be not worth having" explains Richard

"Yes, you are so right ... they were such special times ... and we should leave them as they were" advises Gerry

"We can both agree on that one" replies Richard (Laughs)

LOVE, MUSIC AND DANCING

Bradford Mecca Locarno ... 1967 ... The Swinging Sixties ... Tamla Motown ...

It's the heyday when boy used to meet girl and set way before the Internet and Speed dating!

This is how it used to be ...

Leeds Tiffany's at the Merrion Centre in the Seventies was also a favourite haunt of everyone back then.

It was a crowd puller with its unique Polynesian Night Club ...

Bali Hai ... was the place to be when the sun goes down!

Six individual stories of LOVE, MUSIC, AND MEMORIES ... accompanied with lots of dancing!

You are invited to experience a time when everything was about fashion, music and when girls met boys and vice versa!

THIS IS THE MECCA STORY ...

SAM AND MARTIN'S STORY

Friday night, mid-Autumn ... it's cold and wet outside but there's a new place to go ... Bradford Mecca Locarno on Manningham Lane.

It's a huge venue with a big dance floor.

It has a records section with a resident DJ and the Bobby Brook Band playing "Live" to the hits of the day!

Let the story begin ... 1967 ... in the Jones household in Shipley ...

"Where's my white shirt, Mum?" asks Martin (Smiles)

"It's with your suit and tie in the wardrobe, Martin" advises Mum (Shouts)

"Thanks, Mum" replies Martin (Laughs)

Martin is 6 feet tall, has brown hair, blue eyes, handsome ...

"That lad is always on the go" adds Dad (Looks concerned)

"Oh, he's growing up, Don" replies Mum (Smiling)

"Let him have his fun while he can" adds Mum

"Fun ... is that what they call it today, Blanch?" asks Don (Laughs)

"You know what I mean" advises Blanch (Smiles)

Minutes later, Martin joins his Mum and Dad, and younger sister, Katie for tea ...

"Sorry, I'll have to dash" advises Martin (Grabs a sandwich)

"What at this time?" asks Dad (Looks serious)

"It's 6.30pm ... why the rush, Martin?" replies Mum (Looks at clock)

"I've arranged to meet my mates outside the Library Theatre in Bradford" explains Martin (Smiles)

"Go on, lad" advises Mum (Smiling)

With a kiss on the cheek, Martin is out of the door ...

"Why can't I go, Mum?" asks Katie (Looks puzzled)

"Your only 12 ... plenty of time for that love" advises Dad (Smiling)

"And that will come soon enough my girl" adds Mum (Smiles)

Katie is about five feet tall, has long dark hair, brown eyes, and very slim. She is still growing in stature!

Meanwhile at another household in Dewsbury is Samantha, a pretty, slim brunette, just 18, with blue striking eyes ...

"Where are you going tonight, Samantha?" asks Dad

(Smiles)

"I'm going with Christine to Bradford Mecca" advises Sam (Smiling)

Christine is also 18, 5ft 6, has long blonde hair, blue eyes with a curvaceous figure.

"How are you going to get home?" asks Mum (Looks concerned)

"Christine's dad will bring us back" explains Sam

"So, you can rest easy" adds Sam (Smiles)

"Yes, I suppose we can, love" replies Dad (Smiling)

Pop music is playing on the radio in the background ...

Sam is dressed in a while blouse and a typical Sixties mini skirt ...

"Whatever you do ... don't bend over" advises Dad (Looks serious)

"Why, Dad?" asks Sam (Looks puzzled)

"They will be able to see what you had for breakfast if you do" adds Dad (Laughing)

Sam's older brother, James walks into the living room ...

"It's OK, Sam ... I got the same third-degree questions when I started going out" advises James (Smiles)

Sam laughs ...

"Well, we were only concerned about your welfare" replies Mum

James kisses his Mum on the cheek ...

"I know, Mum ... and I love you for it" advises James (Waves)

"You too, Dad" adds James (Smiling)

"Where are you going, James?" asks Sam (Smiles)

"We're staying local ... probably the Black Tulip or the John FK" replies James

"Don't get into any trouble, James" advises Mum (Looks concerned)

"Do you remember when we were dating, Tom?" asks Mum (Smiles)

"Yes of course I do, Blanch" replies Tom (Laughs)

"Here we go" adds James (Laughs)

"Well, I will be off now, Mum and Dad" advises Sam (Peck on cheeks)

"Don't forget ... take care tonight" advises Mum (Looks concerned)

"Yes, remember what I always tell you" adds Dad

"Make sure you come back with your tail between your legs" explains Dad (Smiles)

"We will, Dad ... don't worry" replies James (Smiling)

It's now early evening ... the Bradford Mecca Locarno on Manningham Lane is open for business ...

If you arrive early ... you get in for free!

Sam and Christine arrive at the venue just before

9pm ...

Both step into the large Foyer ...

"Just in time" greets Keith (General Manager)

"It's free until 9pm" adds Keith (Smiling)

Sam and Christine enter the aptly named LADIES BOUDOIR and hand over their coats to the Cloakroom attendant ...

The STAG ROOM is to the left ... HENS is on the right ...

The Ladies Boudoir is dimly lit with lots of mirrors on various walls.

You can see yourself from every angle.

Outside, through a set of doors, is a tall glass unit advertising what's coming "next week" in the prestigious venue.

Sam and Christine stop to read the display ...

"Look, I fancy that" advises Christine (Smiling)

"It's a typical Sixties dance with a Fancy Dress theme" adds Christine

"Let's see what happens tonight first, Chris" replies Sam (Smiles)

Sam and Christine begin to walk towards the left of the glass cased unit.

A Coffee Bar themed area backs on to the glass unit. It serves burgers and coffee. It overlooks the enormous dance floor.

There are several staircases down to the next level.

The balcony runs all the way around the dance floor. At the back of the stage area there is a bar. Another bar can be located on the ground floor.

The Bobby Brook Band are playing "live" to popular hits of the day ...

Sam and Christine decide to sit on the balcony and look down from a table through the railings on to the dance floor.

The venue starts to fill up with lots of other revelers ...

The revolving stage changes from the "live" Band to a DJ playing records of the day.

The change over music is Booker T and the MG's "Time is Tight"

The DJ begins to play several upbeat Tamla Motown hits ...

"Oh, I love this" advises Christine (Smiling)

Sam and Christine take to the stairs and walk on to the huge dance floor. It starts to fill up quickly with lots of other dancers.

The music is playing loud ...

Dancing around handbags is the order of the day ... for girls!

Christine is wearing an eye catching psychedelic mini dress ...

It's not long before they are being prepositioned ...

"May we have this dance?" asks a voice

EVERLASTING LOVE

Christine motions that it's OK to join her and Sam ...

The DJ changes the records to Tamla and Soul music ...

"Are you girls from here?" asks the voice

"No, are you?" asks Christine (Smiles)

"Bradford" replies the other voice ...

Christine whispers to Sam that she is not happy with her partner!

Both decide to come off the dance floor ...

"We're going for a drink" advises Christine (Points to bar)

"See you later" reply both men (Look stunned)

Sam and Christine retrace their steps back to the table on the balcony ...

"Well, that was a waste of time, Sam" advises Christine (Looks miffed)

Martin and his mate Johnny enter the balcony area ... both are wearing the latest Sixties gear ...

Sam and Christine notice their sudden arrival ...

"Now, they can have me anytime" drools Christine

"Christine" replies Sam (Looks shocked)

"Let's see where tonight takes us" adds Sam (Sounds serious)

Martin and Johnny order at the bar ...

"Well, what do you think?" asks Martin (Smiles)

"It's a nice place but I hope it's not going to mecca me

sick" quips Johnny (Both Laughing)

"Yea, me too, mate" replies Martin (Still Laughing)

Suddenly, Sam and Christine pass by ...

"Cop your eyes on those two bobby dazzlers" advises Johnny (Eyes popping out of sockets)

"They can have the top off my egg any day" adds Martin (Both laugh)

The music changes over from the DJ to the "live" band ...

Bobby Brook announces ...

"OK, please take your partners for the barn dance" advises Bobby (Smiling)

"That's me out" advises Johnny (Looks sad)

"What about you, Martin?" asks Johnny

"I'm going to give it a go ... I mean how hard can it be?" asks Martin (Sounds optimistic)

"Good luck with that" adds Johnny (Looks amused)

The Band starts up with various numbers ...

It's a long way to Tipperary ... you know that type of music!

Everyone must face off then move on to the next partner ...

It goes on for twenty minutes!

Eventually, Martin rejoins Johnny close to the bar area ...

"I saw you dancing with that bird" advises Johnny (Smiling)

"Which one ... there were so many?" asks Martin (Smiling)

"The blonde ... you know ... the one we saw before" asks Johnny

"Oh, she was all smiles" replies Martin (Looks happy)

"Yea, but did she give you the come on?" asks Johnny (Looks intrigued)

"Possibly" adds Martin (Smiles)

"Well, I say we nab those two when the music changes" advises Johnny

"Yea ... we will, mate" replies Martin (Looks serious)

The Bobby Brook band changes over from the barn dance to more upbeat Sixties pop songs ... they have three singers in the band!

Sam and Christine take to the dance floor ...

"OK, this is our moment ... our opportunity" advises Martin (Smiles)

"Just remember one thing" insists Johnny (Sounds serious)

"What's that?" asks Martin (Looks intrigued)

"If we get the brush off ... go to the next two until we get accepted" instructs Johnny

"Don't come off the dance floor ... that way it won't look so obvious" adds Johnny (Looks serious)

"OK, Kemosabe" replies Martin (Laughs)

"Hi Ho Silver" advises Johnny (Both Laughing)

Martin and Johnny venture over towards Sam and Christine ...

"May we have this dance, please?" asks Johnny (Smiles)

This provokes a big smile from Sam and Christine!

A wink and a glint in the eye from Martin and Johnny!

"Do you come here often?" asks Martin (Smiling)

"It's our first night" replies Sam (Big Smile)

"What about you?" asks Sam (Smiles)

"It's our first night too" advises Martin (Smiling)

The music changes over to records and to the DJ ... Time is Tight is now playing ...

"Well, it could be your lucky night, love" adds Sam

"Yours too ... if you play your cards right" replies Martin (Winks)

The DJ plays lots of Soul and Tamla music ...

"He is playing a lot of Tamla tonight" advises Christine (Smiling)

"Oh, he is also the DJ at the Hole in the Wall" explains Johnny

"Call me Chris" advises Christine (Kisses Johnny)

"Wow you're a fast worker, love" adds Johnny (Looks stunned)

"Well, no use in beating about the bush ... I fancy you" replies Chris

"Do you fancy me?" asks Chris (Big Smile)

"Yea, of course I do" adds Johnny (Smiles)

"Have you ever been to the Hole in the Wall, Chris?" asks Johnny

"No ... have you?" asks Chris (Looks inquisitive)

"Yea ... loads of times" replies Johnny

"Maybe you can take me there" asks Chris (Looks intrigued)

"Yea, why not" adds Johnny (Looks pleased)

Sam and Christine pair off with Martin and Johnny ...

It's now the slow records section ...

The DJ plays several love songs from the Swinging Sixties ...

"I love this song" advises Sam (Winks at Martin)

Martin puts his arms around Sam and holds her close ...

"Yea, me too, Sam" replies Martin (Starts Kissing Sam)

"Well, have you had a good night, Martin?" asks Sam (Smiles)

"Only since I met you, love" replies Martin (Smiling)

"Oh, I bet you say that to all the girls" adds Sam

"No ... you're my first" explains Martin (Looks serious)

"What about you Christine?" asks Sam (Turns around)

"We're making a date to go to the Hole in the Wall next Saturday" advises Christine (Smiling)

"Count us both in" reply Martin and Sam (Looks serious)

"It's a date then" adds Johnny (Smiling)

THE WALL FLOWER STORY

Derek is an Accountant, and he lives in Bradford.

Beryl is a bit of a "boffin" and works at the University of Bradford close to the City Centre.

They both have something in common ... they are both loners and go to the Mecca on Manningham Lane on a Saturday night.

Derek and Beryl are well dressed but never seem to find a partner!

Is their luck about to change ... is this their lucky night?

Will they wait for the last dance for the Wallflower's traditional move?

A typical Saturday night ...

Derek is at his Mum's house prior to going to the Mecca ... on his own ...

"It's time you found yourself a wife my lad" advises his Mum (Looks serious)

"Mum ... I'm over 40 ... I was a lad long ago" replies Derek (Sounds serious)

"You know what I mean, Derek" replies Mum (Looks concerned)

"Anyway ... who would want me?" adds Derek

"Someone will ... come on Derek assert yourself" advises Mum (Sounds serious)

Derek is five feet 10, has brown hair and green eyes, a bit boring, wears glasses and not particularly good looking.

Derek wears clothes from "Greenwoods" and is a bit of a square, predictable and a real fuddy-duddy!

Beryl lives on her own, close to Bradford University. She is a loner, spends most of her time in a laboratory. Beryl is not extremely attractive but dreams of meeting the one. Beryl is also very shy!

Beryl plans to go to the Mecca Locarno on Manningham Lane later.

Beryl's friend Margaret calls her on the telephone ...

"Hi Beryl ... it's Margaret" greets the voice

"Oh, hi, Margaret" replies Beryl

"Just wondered if you are, OK?" asks Margaret (Sounds serious)

"Yes, I'm fine, Margaret ... what about you?" asks Beryl

"Yes, I'm great, thanks" replies Margaret

"So, what are you doing later?" asks Margaret (Sounds

intrigued)

"I thought that I would go to the Mecca on Manningham Lane, later, Margaret" advises Beryl (Sounds positive)

"I always thought that you hated dancing?" adds Margaret (Sounds stunned)

"Well, I do ... but how will I ever meet someone if I don't try?" explains Beryl (Sighs)

"What's the plan?" asks Margaret (Sounds inquisitive)

"I'm just going to see what happens" advises Beryl

"You never know ... tonight could be your lucky night" replies Margaret

"Yes, you never know ... it just might be" adds Beryl (Sounds excited)

It's now 8.30pm, Derek has arrived at the Mecca Locarno on Manningham Lane.

Derek is wearing a blue jacket, tie with blue shirt, black trousers, and his trademark "specs"

The Ballroom starts to fill up with lots of revelers ...

No one gives Derek a second glance!

Derek asks no one to dance ... all night!

This is Derek's usual way of life ... someone who just doesn't fit into a normal routine!

A square peg in a round hole to be precise!

The DJ plays several upbeat Sixties pop songs ...

Everyone is on the dance floor except for Derek ...

Beryl has now arrived at the Mecca, and she soon enters the Ballroom.

Beryl is five foot 8, brunette, not very pretty, presentable ...

Several men ask Beryl to dance ... but she declines!

The DJ changes the tempo of the music, and everyone piles on to the dance floor ...

The place is buzzing ... the dance floor is packed ...

Derek decides to try his luck with someone sat in the lower Ballroom.

Beryl is sat at a dimly lit table on the balcony alone ...

"May I have this dance?" asks Derek (Looks embarrassed)

"No thanks" replies a young woman (Looks away and laughs)

Derek doesn't give up and tries again ...

"Can I have this dance?" asks Derek (Sounds sincere)

"Oh, I've just sat down love, and my feet are killing me ... maybe later?" replies a woman in her forties (Smiles)

It's yet another brush off and put down!

Derek decides to take a walk around the dance floor then climbs the stairs up to the balcony.

Derek notices Beryl sat on her own but passes her by ...

Beryl eventually plucks up the courage to dance ...

She says to herself ...

"The next time someone asks me to dance, I'll do it" advises Beryl

Beryl is in her late thirties, shy and introverted. She needs to come out of her shell before it's too late!

The revolving stage changes over from the DJ to the "Live" band ... Bobby Brook and his fellow musicians are playing "Time is Tight"

Bobby's band has three singers, 2 females and a male ...

The band starts to play a medley of upbeat pop songs ...

Everyone is on the dance floor taking full advantage of the music ...

Derek is well known to several Mecca revelers ...

"There he is" advises a voice (Points)

"Who?" asks another voice (Looks around)

"I don't know his name ... only by sight" advises the girl (Looks serious)

"What about him?" asks the other girl (Looks intrigued)

"He's known as the one who talks to nobody ... no one ever notices him and if they do it doesn't end up well" advises the voice

"It sounds like you know him, Amy?" asks the other

girl (Looks serious)

"No one knows anything about him, only his name, Gayle" advises Amy

"What is he called?" asks Gayle (Looks intrigued)

"Derek" replies Amy (Looks serious)

"Well, that's boring for a start" laughs Gayle

"So, how come you know him?" asks Gayle

"I remember him from School" replies Amy (Looks serious)

"What was he like then?" asks Gayle (Looks intrigued)

"Weird" adds Amy (Looks concerned)

The change over from the band back to the DJ takes place ... everyone is dancing to YMCA by the Village People ...

The dance floor is packed with lots of people all doing the actions and routine to the popular song ...

After lots of Soul and Tamla Motown the stage revolves again to find Bobby Brook and his Band ...

Bobby makes an announcement ...

"Please take your partners for the barn dance" advises Bobby (Smiling)

It goes on for twenty minutes and various partners change several times.

Beryl gets asked to dance ...

After a few dances, Beryl decides to go back to her

table on the balcony ...

"Stuck up so and so" advises her dancing partner (Looks miffed)

"I thought you were in there" replies his mate (Looks puzzled)

"No such luck" replies the dancing partner (Looks moody)

"What are we waiting for ... there's plenty more fish in the sea" adds his mate (Sounds philosophical)

"Yea ... as good as ever came out of it" laughs the dancing partner

"Come on we'll try our luck over here" replies his mate (Points)

Beryl makes her way to the bar.

It's fast approaching 11pm ...

Beryl is again propositioned at the bar!

"Can I buy you a drink, love?" asks a male voice (Winks)

"No thanks ... my boyfriend's waiting for me" replies Beryl (Smiles)

Beryl uses this line to put them down and put them off pestering her!

Derek is on the prowl but getting laughed at for his appearance ...

"He would look a lot better with long hair" advises a woman

"And a new set of gear" remark a couple of girls (Laughing)

"Maybe we would give him a second glance then?" advises one of the girls (Points)

"Maybe" replies the other girl (Smiling)

Derek is very reserved and not the trendy type!

Derek really has a very boring image ...

Beryl notices Derek being put down and is not surprised why.

It's now fast approaching Midnight.

The Bobby Brook band has just finished their set.

The stage revolves and the DJ takes over and he starts to play "smooch" records ...

Derek notices Beryl and decides to ask her for a dance ...

"Can I have this dance?" asks a polite Derek (Smiles)

Beryl feels sorry for Derek and agrees to go on the dance floor with him ...

"OK, love, thank you, I will" replies Beryl (Smiling)

"I'm Derek" greets Derek (Smiles)

"Beryl" replies Beryl (Smiling)

"I'm from Bradford ... you?" asks Derek (Sounds serious)

"Me too, love" replies Beryl (Laughs)

Derek asks the most frequently used question that

everybody asks ...

"Do you come here often, Beryl?" asks Derek

"No, it's my first time, Derek" replies Beryl

The conversation flows and it's clear to see that Derek has something in common with Beryl!

"What do you do, Derek?" asks Beryl (Sounds inquisitive)

"I'm an accountant ... you?" replies Derek

"I work at the University" advises Beryl

"What do you do there?" asks Derek

"I am in research" explains Beryl

"A bit of a boffin then?" adds Derek (Smiles)

Beryl laughs at Derek's comical remark ...

"Do you fancy a drink after our dance?" asks Derek (Looks shy)

"Don't mind if I do, love" replies Beryl (Smiling)

Derek and Beryl head for the balcony and find a dimly lit table overlooking the dance floor ...

"What would you like to drink, Beryl?" asks Derek

"A lager and black please, Derek" replies Beryl (Smiles)

"Coming up" adds Derek (Smiling)

Derek is away from the table for several minutes as the bar is packed.

He notices Beryl has been asked to dance again but she refuses!

Derek eventually returns to the table and passes over Beryl's drink ...

"So, have you enjoyed your first time here, Beryl?" asks Derek (Sounds sincere)

"Yes, I've loved it ... but I am a bit of a recluse normally" explains Beryl

"Yea, I know what you mean ... so am I" adds Derek (Smiles)

"Why haven't you met someone here before?" asks Beryl (Looks intrigued)

"I suppose it's because I am a bit shy and reserved" replies Derek

"Me too ... nothing wrong with that" advises Beryl (Laughs)

"So, do you live alone?" asks Derek (Looks inquisitive)

Beryl is careful with her answer ...

"I've got a flat mate" replies Beryl (Looks cautious)

"You?" asks Beryl (Sounds intrigued)

"I live with my aging Mum" explains Derek (Smiles)

"Maybe we can have a night out sometime" asks Derek

"Maybe" replies Beryl (Smiles)

"What about next Wednesday?" asks Derek (Sounds hopeful)

"What about it?" replies Beryl (Laughs)

"Oh, I see your asking me out?" adds Beryl (Sounds

stunned)

"OK, I would love to" explains Beryl (Smiling)

Derek is over the moon and can't contain his delight ...

"OK, I will meet you on Wednesday outside of the library theatre at 8pm" advises Derek

"It's a date" replies Beryl (Smiling)

BALI HAI

Tiffany's Leeds in the Seventies ...

Bali Hai is a nightclub within a nightclub in the Merrion Centre.

It is Polynesian and it has been decked out with plastic palm trees and typical basket weave tables and chairs ...

A contest is taking place for the best dressed male and the best dressed female ...

Two young men are in conversation close to the Bali Hai bar area ...

"Two beers please" orders Mike (Smiling)

"Pints or halves?" asks one of the bar staff (Smiles)

"Pints" replies Mike (Smiling)

"That will be six pounds" advises a bar lady

Mike hands over the other pint to his mate, Ben ...

"It's a bit pricey in here, Mike" advises Ben (Looks concerned)

"You said it, mate" adds Mike (Laughs)

"That's how they get you in these places" quips Mike

EVERLASTING LOVE

Ben is six feet tall, has brown hair and blue eyes, in his early twenties, wearing powder blue 24-inch bell bottom trousers and a shirt to match with a jacket and tie.

Mike is five foot 10, has brown hair, brown eyes, also in his early twenties, he is wearing a similar outfit, 24-inch green bell bottom trousers, a green shirt with matching tie and a jacket.

You can't get into the Mecca without a tie or a jacket!

It's one of the main rules and stipulations for entry.

The Bali Hai is an intimate dimly lit nightclub. It has fish nets hanging from the ceiling with lanterns and it has two small dance floors. The atmosphere, artificial lighting and palm trees adds to the nostalgic feel of a Polynesian night out.

Lucy and Debbie enter the Bali Hai nightclub ... and it's not long before they are being eyed by several males ...

"Don't look now but I think we're about to be approached" advises Lucy (Winks)

The DJ is playing several Seventies disco hits ...

Mike and Ben go steaming in ...

Lucy and Debbie are both in their twenties and of average height, blue eyed blondes, wearing miniskirts topped off with blue almost see through blouses!

"May we have this dance?" asks Mike (Sounds smooth)

"Yea, why not?" replies Debbie (Smiling)

Ben asks Lucy to dance ...

Lucy smiles and accepts ...

The girls are spun the usual chat up lines but are not taken in by their banter ... they decide to head for the bar!

"Well, that went down like a ton of bricks" advises Ben (Looks puzzled)

"You can't win them all, Ben" quips Mike (Laughing)

"The night is young ... there's plenty more to go at, Ben" adds Mike (Sounds philosophical)

The DJ makes an announcement ...

"We're having a contest later to find the best dressed male and female ... see Alan at the door if you want to participate" advises the DJ (Pointing)

The DJ is now playing several Soul and Tamla records on the double deck turntables.

Mike starts to chat up a couple of girls just off the dance floor ...

"This is my mate, Ben" advises Mike (Smiling)

"Hi" replies one of the girls (Smiles)

"We're Kate and Lauren" replies Kate (Big Smile)

Kate is five foot eight, has green eyes, an attractive brunette ...

Lauren is 6ft tall, has curly blonde hair and blue eyes, also extremely attractive ...

"Do you both live in Leeds, girls?" asks Mike (Looks inquisitive)

EVERLASTING LOVE

"Yea ... we're both Nurses at the Leeds General Infirmary" replies Kate (Smiling)

"What about you?" asks Lauren (Smiles)

"Oh, we're Brain Surgeons" quips Mike (All Laughing)

"What do you really do?" asks Kate (Looks inquisitive)

"We both work in finance in the city" explains Ben (Smiles)

"Hey, fancy a dance, girls?" asks Mike (Points to dance floor)

"Yea, why not?" replies Kate (Smiling)

The DJ is now playing several hits from the charts ...

"Oh, I love this" advises Lauren (Smiles)

"Do you fancy yourself as a bit of a groover, Ben?" asks Kate (Winks)

"I'll give it a go, love" replies Ben (Laughs)

The DJ suddenly makes another announcement ...

"OK, just to advise that we have now found several contestants for the best dressed male and female contest ... more later" ends the DJ

"Where's Lauren?" asks Kate (Looks around)

"And where's Mike?" adds Ben (Looks over to the bar)

Several contestants come forward ...

"Why it's ..." advises Kate (Looks stunned)

"Lauren and Mike" adds Ben (Looks equally stunned)

The DJ stops the music and starts to grill the

contestants ...

"So, have you both being going out long?" asks the DJ (Smiles)

"We've only just met, tonight" replies Mike (Laughs)

"Wow ... quick workers" quips the DJ (All Laughing)

"When's the wedding?" adds the DJ (All Laughing)

"Well, you both look the part ... best of luck" adds the DJ (Smiles)

Then it's on to another couple ...

"Well, that took me by surprise, Kate" advises Ben (Looks shocked)

"Me too, Ben" replies Kate (Smiling)

"Tell me more about yourself, Kate?" asks Ben (Looks inquisitive)

"Well" adds Kate (Starts to go into raptures)

The DJ suddenly makes another announcement ...

"And the winners are?" advises the DJ (Drum roll)

"Lauren and Mike" replies the DJ (Smiling)

"Well, what have you got to say?" asks the DJ (Laughs)

Mike and Lauren both look speechless!

"OK ... while you're thinking of what to say" adds the DJ

"Here's a double play of the Gibson Brothers" explains the DJ

"By the way ... are we all invited to the wedding?"

laughs the DJ

Mike and Lauren are stunned by that remark!

The dance floor quickly fills up ...

A sudden loud "bleeping" noise stops proceedings ...

"Sorry, I'll have to go" advises Lauren (Looks serious)

"Where?" asks Mike (Looks concerned)

"Back to Leeds General Infirmary" replies Lauren

"Are you wanted in Casualty?" asks Mike (Looks puzzled)

"Something like that, darling" adds Lauren (Looks concerned)

Lauren kisses Mike on the lips and gives him her telephone number ...

"Call me ...OK?" asks Luren (Smiling)

Lauren motions to Kate that she will be back later ...

"Since when did Nurses have pagers?" asks Mike (Looks stunned)

"Never" advises Kate (Smiles)

"Lauren is a Doctor at the LGI" explains Kate (Sounds serious)

"We thought you were both Nurses" advises Ben (Looks stunned)

"We know what you thought" replies Kate (Looks cautious)

Suddenly alarms start to go off in Tiffany's and Bali

Hai ...

The DJ makes a serious announcement ...

"OK, we have an incident ... everyone must leave the building and go on to the concourse until advised" explains the DJ (Sounds serious)

The Police arrive followed by the Fire Brigade and pandemonium ensues!

The Merrion Centre is cordoned off ... there is no way in or out of the complex.

Thirty minutes later ...

Mike and Ben assure Kate all is OK.

Suddenly, Kate's "beeper" goes off ...

"Don't tell me, you're a doctor too?" asks Ben (Looks serious)

"Afraid so ... I'll have to go ... here's my phone number, Ben ... call me" replies Kate (Kisses Ben on the lips)

Kate leaves Bali Hai and heads straight for the LGI.

The DJ makes another announcement and gives the "all clear"

The revelers return into Tiffany's and the Bali Hai ...

Dancing resumes ...

"Well, that's twice we've missed out tonight, Ben" advises Mike (Looks puzzled)

"It's been exciting though" replies Ben (Smiles)

"You can say that again, Ben" adds Mike (Smiling)

It turns out that an incident had taken place inside Tiffany's, although no specific details were given ...

The DJ advises that it is "Party time" and tries to get everyone back on the dance floor and into the spirit of the evening!

The mood is suddenly uplifting ... everyone seems to have forgotten the night's other events ...

Mike and Ben are back on the prowl, and decide to try their luck in Tiffany's ...

The "live" Band is now playing the barn dance ...

"Oh, I hate this" advises Mike (Looks stunned)

"Let's wait it out" replies Ben (Smiles)

"Come on Ben, I'll get the beers in" adds Mike (Points to bar)

Ben notices a dark-haired female with her head down at a table and decides to go in for the kill ...

"Can I have this dance, love?" asks Ben (Smiling)

Suddenly, a head goes up and tells him where to go!

It's a man!

Ben is taken aback and tells Mike his story ...

"Well, it serves you right for asking" laughs Mike

The resident DJ makes an appearance and the music switches to upbeat pop music ...

"Right, come on, Ben ... time to make another move" advises Mike

"Oh, remember one thing, Ben" adds Mike (Sounds serious)

"What's that, Mike?" asks Ben (Looks puzzled)

"If we get a refusal, we will just go to the next two until we get a dance" replies Mike (Smiling)

"OK, I will remember that Mike" laughs Ben

The dance floor is packed and lots of girls are dancing to Wig Wam Bam by the Sweet.

All the girls are doing the same actions and routines to the popular song!

"What about those two?" asks Mike (Pointing)

"Too old" replies Ben (Laughs)

"OK, what about those?" adds Mike (Points to another two girls)

"Too young" adds Ben (Smiling)

"Is there anyone who is, OK?" asks Mike (Looks stunned)

"I'm still smitten with my doctor" replies Ben (Sighs)

"Yea, me too" adds Mike (Both look serious)

"Who knows, we may bump into them again one day" advises Mike

"Well, that's a dead cert" explains Ben (Smiling)

"I've got Kate's phone number … she seemed keen" adds Ben

"And I've got Lauren's number … she seemed to be the

same" replies Mike

"Come on, let's go for it" adds Mike (Both Smiling)

Ben and Mike decide to call Kate and Lauren next day ...

All four decide on a double date in Leeds at the earliest opportunity!

NEW VENTURE SINGLES

Terry sees an advertisement in the Personal Section of the Yorkshire Evening Post ...

NEW VENTURE SINGLES DANCE IN THE MERRION BANQUETING SUITE ... 8.30PM TILL LATE ... EVERY THURSDAY EVENING ... SEE YOU THERE!!!

Will Terry dare attend the New Venture Singles dance?

Thursday ... Terry decides to go to the New Venture Singles dance and arrives in good time at the Merrion Centre in Leeds.

Terry parks his car in the Merrion Hotel car park and makes his way down into the Merrion Centre.

Terry asks for directions ...

EVERLASTING LOVE

"Excuse me, can you tell me where the Merrion Banqueting suite is?" asks Terry (Smiles)

"Aye, lad ... take the flight of stairs up next to Le Phonographique" advises a passing gentleman (Points the way)

"Then what?" asks Terry (Looks puzzled)

"Follow the balcony to the end ... you'll see two doors on the right ... that's the Merrion Banqueting suite" explains the gentleman

"Thanks" replies Terry (Smiling)

"Your very welcome, lad" replies the gentleman (Laughs)

Terry negates the stairs up to the Merrion Suite and comes across the "Stags" room and Cloak room.

It is dimly lit, and there are mirrors on all the walls.

It boasts a typical Mecca decor of the era with plenty of flocked wallpaper.

After doing the "Fonz" impression in the mirrors, Terry enters the Banqueting Suite ...

A man and woman are sat at a table with a cash box ...

"Good evening" greets a voice (Smiles)

"Welcome to the New Venture Singles Club" greets the gentleman (Smiles)

"That'll be 50p" adds the lady (Smiles)

Terry pays the entry fee ...

"Does it get busy in here?" asks Terry (Looks

concerned)

"Yes, it will later ... you're a bit soon" replies the lady (Smiling)

The Banqueting Suite has a long bar to the right. It has a mirrored background and mirror panels on all columns and walls making it look bigger than it is.

It has dimly lit tables with red lampshades and a small disco type of dance floor on the left in front of the resident DJ.

Soothing middle of the road music is playing in the background ...

Terry meanders over to the bar ...

"What'll it be?" asks the bar manager (Smiles)

"Half a lager, please" replies Terry (Smiling)

"Coming up" replies the bar manager

Suddenly, someone else arrives ... and joins Terry at the bar ...

"Hi, I'm Martin" greets the voice (Both shake hands)

"Terry" replies Terry (Smiles)

"Have you been here before, Terry?" asks Martin (Sounds inquisitive)

"No ... first night for me" replies Terry

"Oh ... you'll enjoy it tonight" advises Martin (Sounds sincere)

"What's it like?" asks Terry (Looks puzzled)

"A bit grab a granny" laughs Martin

"Oh, I see" replies Terry (Looks stunned)

"Don't be so choosy ... you'll pull tonight" explains Martin

"What about you, Martin?" asks Terry

"Oh, I know the ropes ... it's nailed on here" quips Martin (Smiles)

The Banqueting Suite starts to fill up with the usual loners and "Wall flower" types ... but then enter two stunners!

"Oh, I like mine" quips Martin (Smiles)

"Mines not bad either" laughs Terry

"OK, wait till they get on the dance floor" advises Martin

"Then we'll make our move" adds Martin (Smiling)

"Are you a regular here, Martin?" asks Terry

"Yea ... you could say that" replies Martin

"I come here in between going to Tiffany's on Friday and Saturday nights" explains Martin

"This is a guaranteed, nailed on pulling night" adds Marin (Laughs)

"You can't fail" replies Martin (Looks smug)

Terry is stunned at what Martin has to say and how he just gets on with it ...

"Why?" asks Terry (Looks puzzled)

"They are so grateful" replies Martin (Looks serious)

"Is it because their oldies?" asks Terry

"Yea, that's it" explains Martin

The DJ changes the music to upbeat pop music ...

Martin and Terry decide to get on the dance floor ...

"Right, Terry ... it's time to make our move" advises Martin (Motions to dance floor)

"OK, I'm right behind you" replies Terry (Smiles)

Martin and Terry approach the dance floor ...

They make their introductions ...

"Hi ... I'm Martin ... this is Terry" advises Martin (Smiling)

"Natalie and Amber" reply the girls (Big Smile)

Terry seems to have pulled ...

"So, Amber ... have you been here before?" asks Terry (Smiles)

"No, it's my first time here" replies Amber (Smiling)

"I like it though" adds Amber

Natalie is five foot 10, in her forties, has green eyes and brown wavy hair, quite attractive.

Amber is five foot 8, blue eyes, looks to be in her twenties, has long dark hair and looks innocent ...

"Are you both sisters?" asks Martin (Smiles)

Natalie winks across to Amber ...

"Yea, we are sisters" replies Natalie (Smiling)

"I thought so ... I can see the resemblance" replies Terry

At the end of the night Terry and Martin swap phone numbers with Natalie and Amber ...

"I will be in touch, love" advises Terry (Smiles)

"Yea, OK" replies Natalie (Smiles)

Terry kisses Amber on the lips ...

Several days later, Terry decides to call Amber from the local red phone box for a date ...

Terry dials the number ...

"Hello" greets a voice

"Can I talk to Amber, please?" asks Terry (Sounds polite)

"Who is it?" asks the voice (Sounds serious)

"Terry from the New Venture ... remember?" asks Terry

"Oh, hello Terry ... it's Natalie" replies the voice

"Hi, Natalie ... is Amber there?" asks Terry (Sounds sincere)

"You do know she is only 16, don't you?" asks Natalie (Sounds serious)

Terry is stunned ...

"Oh, no ... but I do now" replies Terry (Sounds stunned)

"Sorry" replies Terry (Sounds embarrassed)

Terry replaces the receiver and leaves the red call box ...

It's the following week at the New Venture Singles dance in the Banqueting Suite in the Merrion Centre ...

Terry tells Martin of his brush with the girl ...

Martin laughs ...

"Well, look at this way ... at least you didn't pull a granny" advises Martin (Both Laughing)

"Better luck next time, pal" adds Martin (Smiles)

The DJ starts to broaden the music and plays several party hits ... more take to the dance floor ...

Tony Christie's Is this the way to Amarillo is now playing ...

Martin starts to sing ...

"Is this the way to Amarillo ... every night I've been stuffing my pillow" (Laughing)

"Come on, Terry ... do you see those two over there?" asks Martin (Pointing)

"OK, let's make ourselves known" adds Martin (Smiles)

Terry and Martin steam in ...

"May we have this dance, love?" asks Martin (Smiles)

"Yea, why not" replies a voice (Smiling)

"Hi, I'm Melanie ... she's Jenny" advises Melanie

(Smiles)

"Hi, Terry and Martin" replies Jenny (Big Smile)

They both ask the usual Question ...

"Do you come here often, love?" asks Martin (Sounds sincere)

"Now and again" replies Jenny (Smiling)

Melanie is a tall blonde with striking looks ... Jenny is also tall, has long wavy brunette hair and attractive ...

"You remind me of someone" advises Terry (Smiles)

"Who?" replies Jenny (Looks inquisitive)

"I don't know but someone for sure" adds Terry

"Someone you know?" asks Jenny (Smiling)

"No, not really" replies Terry (Looks puzzled)

"OK, I'll put you out of your misery" adds Jenny (Laughs)

"I'm frequently told that I look like MARTI CAINE" explains Jenny (Poses)

"I agree ... you are, love" advises Terry (Smiling)

"You look like someone too" replies Jenny (Smiles)

"Who?" asks Terry (Looks puzzled)

"Shoestring" advises Jenny (Laughs)

"Eddie Shoestring on television" explains Jenny (Smiling)

"Well, I suppose I do have a similar Tash and bobbed hair" replies Terry (Sounds stunned)

"Yea, and your bootlace tie" adds Jenny

"See, we have something in common already" laughs Jenny

The DJ changes to upbeat Seventies disco records ...

"Are you from Leeds, Marti ... sorry Jenny?" asks Terry (Looks embarrassed)

Jenny laughs ...

"Roundhay" replies Jenny (Winks)

"What do you do?" asks Terry (Sounds intrigued)

"I'm a hairdresser ... I own my own business, love" advises Jenny (Smiling)

"You?" asks Jenny (Looks inquisitive)

"I work in finance" replies Terry (Looks serious)

Martin motions to Terry ...

"We're going for a drink, mate" advises Martin (Winks)

Melanie and Martin start to leave the dance floor ...

"Do you want to join me?" asks Terry

"Why, are you falling apart?" quips Jenny (Laughs)

"Very funny" laughs Terry

"Yea, we will join you for a drink" replies Melanie (Smiles)

The bar area is now remarkably busy ...

"We're just going to powder our noses, love" advises Jenny (Smiling)

"You're not going to do a runner on us are you?" asks Terry (Looks anxious)

"We'll be back in a minute ... love" laughs Melanie and Jenny

Several minutes later ... Jenny and Melanie return all "dolled up"

"See ... we're back" quips Mel (Smiling)

The DJ changes over the records to a smooch ...

"Fancy a smooch, Jenny?" asks Terry (Smiles)

"Don't mind if I do, Shoestring" quips Jenny (Laughs)

Melanie and Martin are already on the tiny dance floor ... Jenny and Terry join them ...

Terry's hand holds on to Jenny's bum ...

"Shoestring, I'm surprised at you ... trying to take advantage of an innocent lady" advises Jenny (Looks stunned)

"Innocent?" asks Terry (Smiles)

"Well, I am dressed in all white" explains Jenny (Laughs)

"What would MARTI CAINE have said?" adds Terry (Sounds intrigued)

"She would have said keep your hand on my bum ... you've pulled" advises Jenny (Both laughing)

"Naughty MARTI" quips Terry (Looks stunned)

"What does Jenny say?" asks Terry

GERRY CULLEN

"If you play your cards right ... anything could happen tonight" replies Jenny (Winks)

CHRISTMAS AND NEW YEAR

Christmas Eve, Mecca Locarno Ballroom, Manningham Lane, Bradford.

The scene is set, and the music is vibrant.

Will Angela find the man of her dreams before Christmas?

New Year's Eve, Tiffany's, Leeds ... "Masked Ball"

Will Terry and Martin find love, or will they bump into old flames?

THURSDAY, 2 DAYS BEFORE CHRISTMAS EVE ...

Sophie and Angela are in conversation about their plans for Christmas ...

"What have you got planned for Christmas, Sophie?" asks Angela (Smiles)

"Oh, the usual family affair ... what about you, Angela?" asks Sophie (Looks inquisitive)

"I'm hoping to have a little adventure" replies Angela

Sophie is five foot 4, has brown eyes, brunette, and attractive.

Angela is five foot 8, has blue eyes, shoulder length blonde hair, and attractive.

"What type of adventure, Ang?" asks Sophie (Looks stunned)

"I'm hoping to meet someone before Christmas" explains Angela (Smiles)

"That's my dream, Soph" adds Angela (Looks serious)

"How?" asks Sophie (Looks in awe)

"Well, if we play our cards right, we might meet someone on Christmas Eve ... who knows" explains Angela (Looks excited)

"We?" asks Sophie (Looks puzzled)

"You and me, love" replies Angela (Both laugh)

"You seem to have got it all mapped out" adds Sophie (Looks stunned)

"Well, I've got us a couple of tickets" replies Angela

"Where?" asks Sophie (Looks inquisitive)

"Bradford Mecca" explains Angela (Looks excited)

"You must have been so sure that I would come" advises Sophie (Looks stunned)

"Oh, I knew you would" laughs Angela

"OK, it's a date" replies Sophie (Both look excited)

SATURDAY 8PM ...
CHRISTMAS EVE ...

Angela and Sophie are dressed for the occasion ... arriving at the Mecca Locarno Ballroom on Manningham Lane.

There is already a long queue outside the venue waiting for the doors to open ...

Sophie is wearing a psychedelic mini dress with high heel boots ...

Angela is in a white mini dress ... looking gorgeous!

Sophie and Angela show their reserved tickets in the foyer and enter the massive ballroom ...

The Bobby Brook Band are playing various Christmas hits "live"

In the mood music to start ... Deck the Halls/Lonely this Christmas/Rudolph the Red nosed Reindeer ...

"Well, it is Christmas" advises Bobby (Smiling)

Angela and Sophie find a table overlooking the huge dance floor ...

Early evening revelers are already starting to get into the Christmas mood ...

Bobby Brook makes an announcement ...

"OK, please take your partners for the barn dance" advises Bobby (Smiling)

"Oh, I hate this" advises Angela (Looks annoyed)

"Can't you do it?" asks Sophie (Looks puzzled)

"Sorry, hon ... I've got two left feet" adds Angela

"What about you, Soph?" asks Angela (Smiling)

"I can just about get round the floor" advises Sophie

A couple of young men decide to try their luck ...

Someone asks Sophie to dance ...

Sophie decides to give it a go!

"What about you?" asks another voice

"What about me?" replies Angela (Looks daggers)

"Sorry I can't do this" adds Angela

"Maybe later then" adds the voice

"Yea ... maybe later" explains Angela (Smiles)

After half an hour of the barn dance the Band start to play "Time is Tight"

Sophie returns to be with Angela ...

"How did you get on, Soph?" asks Angela (Looks intrigued)

"Oh, we changed partners a few times" replies Sophie

"Yes, I saw you" adds Angela (Smiling)

"Great it's the changeover" advises Sophie (Looks excited)

The night is split with a "live" Band and a DJ playing the records of the day ...

The DJ plays a Christmas mix of hit records ...

"Right, let's get on the dance floor, Soph" advises Angela (Smiles)

Sophie follows Angela down the flight of stairs on to the next level and both walk on to the huge dance floor ...

It fills quickly and the night suddenly takes off!

"I see the wallflowers are in" advises Angela (Points)

"That's Derek over there" adds Angela

"Do you know him?" asks Sophie (Looks round)

"Everyone knows Derek" explains Angela (Smiles)

"What do you mean, Angela?" asks Sophie

"We see him here most weeks and he is never with anyone" explains Angela

The Christmas hits continue ... Angela notices two men looking at them ...

"Don't look now, Soph ... but here come two chancers" advises Angela

"May we have this dance?" asks a voice

"Yea ... why not?" replies Angela (Smiles)

"Do you come here often?" asks the voice (Sounds sincere)

"Now and again" replies Angela (Smiling)

"I'm Dom ... he's Tony" advises Dom (Smiles)

"I'm Angela ... she's Sophie" adds Angela (Smiling)

Dom is five foot 10, in his early twenties, has brown hair, very slim and attractive.

Tony is 6ft tall, also in his early twenties, has fair hair, slim and attractive.

The DJ changes the music to yet more Christmas hits ...

"We're going to sit down now, lads" advises Angela

"OK ... we'll see you both later" replies Dom (Smiles)

"Bye, Sophie" adds Tony (Waves)

"Bye, hon" replies Sophie (Smiles)

Angela and Sophie head back to the upper balcony and sit at another table overlooking the dance floor ...

"Just as it was getting interesting" advises Sophie (Smiles)

"Treat them mean to keep them keen, Soph" replies Angela (Laughs)

"Don't just settle for the first one that comes along, Sophie ... the night is young" adds Angela (Both smile)

"Let's see what happens" explains Angela

"You've really led a sheltered life, Soph" adds Angela

"Maybe I have" replies Sophie (Smiles)

"Well, it's about to change, love" insists Angela

Suddenly, the DJ announces, "It's PARTY TIME" and a whole lot of hats and balloons come tumbling down from the basket in the ceiling ...

The atmosphere is now clearly geared up for a CHRISTMAS EVE PARTY to remember!

Sophie and Angela are back on the dance floor ...

It's not long before they are both asked for a dance!

Both lads are particularly good looking but are more interested in themselves than the girls ...

"That was a waste of time, Soph" advises Angela (Looks annoyed)

"They loved themselves that's for sure, Ang" replies Sophie (Laughs)

"More like they were both up their own back sides" laughs Angela

"Angela" replies a shocked Sophie

"Who knows what might happen tonight?" adds Angela (Smiles)

Several days later it's NEW YEAR'S EVE at Tiffany's in Leeds ...

Tiffany's is located upstairs in the Merrion Centre.

It is loved by generations of dancers from young and old. It has a large ballroom and a separate "Bali Hai" night club for intimate revelers.

There is also a Banqueting Suite available for hire for private secluded parties!

SATURDAY 31ST DECEMBER
– MASKED BALL ...

FANCY DRESS ...

Terry and Martin are two young men out on the town ...

"Well, tonight's the night ... I can feel it" advises Terry (Smiles)

Terry is 6ft tall, has long brown hair, sideburns, blue eyes, very slim and attractive.

"Yea, me too, mate" replies Martin (Laughs)

Martin is also 6ft tall, has long dark hair, brown eyes, slim and attractive.

"That's what we always say" laughs Terry (Optimistic)

"Well, when it gets to Midnight make sure you are next to a good looker ... then move in for a snog" instructs Martin

"Yea, I'll remember" adds Terry (Laughs)

Terry and Martin meet a good looking blonde in reception ...

Terry starts to chat her up ...

"So, what time do you get off, Ruth?" asks Terry (Smiling)

Ruth smiles ...

Inside of Tiffany's there are lots of would-be revelers getting into the spirit of the occasion.

Some are masked ... many are not!

The dance floor fills up quickly ...

Many are wearing masks ... except for Mike and Ben, two more revelers ...

Suddenly, two masked girls approach them ...

"Wanna dance, lads?" asks a voice

"Yea, why not" replies Mike (Smiling)

"You don't remember us, do you?" asks a voice

"Should we?" replies Ben (Sounds intrigued)

"Yes, of course" adds a second voice

Both girls remove their masks ...

"Lauren ... Kate" advises a stunned Mike and Ben (Both look surprised)

"So, you do remember us?" asks Lauren (Laughs)

"Doctor Lauren" advises Mike (Smiling)

"Doctor Kate" adds Ben (Smiles)

"Why didn't you call me, Ben?" asks Kate (Sounds serious)

"I wanted to ... but I thought you would be busy at the LGI" replies Ben

"I'm always busy there ... so is Lauren ... but we always make time for our boyfriends" explains Kate (Smiling)

"Is that what we are?" asks Mike (Smiles)

"You can be ... if you want to be" explains Lauren (Smiling)

"Come on, it's New Year's Eve ... let's see where the night takes us" advises Mike (Smiling)

Back at Bradford Mecca the New Year's Eve night is in full swing ...

Angela and Sophie have also bumped into Dom and Tony who they first met a week ago ...

"Come on Dom ... let's go for a boogie" advises Angela (Smiles)

"What about Sophie and Tony?" asks Dom (Looks concerned)

"Oh, I'm sure those two lovebirds can get along without us" adds Angela (Kisses Dom)

"We'll join you later" advises Dom (Waves)

"Don't do anything I wouldn't do, Soph" advises Angela (Winks)

"That leaves a lot to the imagination" quips Sophie (Laughs)

The DJ begins to play a mix of Soul and Tamla Motown records ...

Sophie and Tony decide to join Angela and Dom on the huge dance floor ...

It's a full house and the place is buzzing!

It's Midnight ... the music is intimate ...

"Well, Sophie have I made your Christmas?" asks Tony (Smiles)

"Yes, in more ways than one, honey" replies Sophie (Smiling)

"What about you Ang?" asks Sophie (Looks

embarrassed)

"No need to ask them ... they are both snogging" replies Tony

Sophie and Tony look at each other and begin to snog in response!

The DJ stops proceedings and proudly announces the countdown to the end of the old year ...

"HAPPY NEW YEAR" shouts the DJ (Lots of cheering)

There is also lots of kissing everywhere!

Meanwhile, at Tiffany's in Leeds the "Masked Ball" is also counting down to the New Year ...

"OK, everyone ... lets countdown together" announces the DJ

"Ten, nine, eight, seven, six, five, four, three, two ... one .... HAPPY NEW YEAR" shouts the DJ (Lots of cheering)

Mike and Lauren along with Ben and Kate start to snog ...

Suddenly, a call on the microphone by the DJ ...

"Is there a doctor in the house?" shouts the DJ (Sounds concerned)

"Oh no, not again" advises Mike

"Sorry I have to go" advises Lauren

"Me, too" adds Kate

"We shouldn't be too long ... we'll be back" advises Lauren

Both girls kiss Mike and Ben ...

"Don't worry we will be waiting for you" replies Ben and Mike

"I suppose it's something we'll have to get used to mate" advises Mike

"Yes, I guess so" replies Ben (Smiles)

Suddenly, two stunners wish them both a Happy New Year ...

"Sorry, girls we're waiting for our partners" advises Mike

"Shame" replies a young woman (Looks stunned)

"Now that's something that wouldn't have happened a week ago" replies Ben (Both laugh)

LOVE AND MEMORIES ... A COMPANY DANCE STORY

Mid-Summer, Bradford Mecca Locarno ...

Watsons are having their annual dance ... will it be a time for new relationships to develop or hostile take overs?

Friday, Payday ... In the office of Watsons in the city Centre ...

"Are you looking forward to the dance tonight, Muriel?" asks Bob (Work colleague)

"Absolutely Bob, are you, love?" asks Muriel (Smiles)

"Yes, of course ... don't forget to come and have a dance with me, will you?" replies Bob (Winks)

"Of course I won't Bob ... I'll hold you to that, love" advises Muriel (Laughs)

"Are you going, Derek?" asks Muriel (Sounds intrigued)

"Yea ... I'll be there" replies Derek (Smiles)

Sadly, Derek is a resident "Wallflower," but his luck was in recently when he met Beryl ...

"... and I've got a date" adds Derek (Looks excited)

"Really, at last ... I'm so proud of you, Derek" explains Muriel (Smiling)

"What about you two love birds?" asks Muriel

Sixteen-year-olds, Amanda and Tim, newbies of the office ...

"We'll be there" advises Amanda (Smiling)

"... and we're not love birds" replies Tim (Laughing)

"It's going to be fabulous" advises Jonathan (Smiling)

"I think that's taking it a step too far, Jonathan" replies Muriel

"It should be memorable though" advises Jonathan

"Our dances are usually legendary" explains Jonathan

"Yea, for all the wrong reasons" laughs Bob

"Well, everyone must be on their best behaviour tonight" advises Mr. Watson (Owner)

"Yes, Mr. Watson" reply all staff (Smiling)

"Remember, you are all representing the company" adds Mr. Watson (Looks stern)

"We will, Sir" advise Bob and Muriel (Long serving

employees)

Early evening ... a party of 50 strong arrive in a coach outside the Mecca Locarno on Manningham Lane ...

Mr. Watson and his party walk into the Foyer and reception area of the Mecca Locarno ...

"Watsons" advises the MD to the Receptionist (Smiles)

"Please go on through ... our General Manager is waiting to greet you all" advises Barbara (Smiles)

Keith Forbes officially greets Mr. Watson and his employees to the Mecca Locarno ...

"Welcome to the Bradford Mecca Locarno" greets Keith (Smiles)

Both men shake hands ... Keith takes Mr. Watson and his wife on a personal guided tour of the venue.

Dale Watson makes his way into the Ballroom with his wife, Constance ... followed by Watson employees ...

The huge dance floor is already filling up and the Bobby Brook Band are playing "live" on stage ...

The barn dance is in full swing ...

"Oh, I love this" advises Muriel (Smiling)

"Come on, Bob" adds Muriel

"I'm coming, Muriel" laughs Bob

"You'd think those two were married" advises Tim (Smiling)

"They were ... once" replies Derek (Smiles)

"Well, blow me down, I never knew that" replies Tim (Looks stunned)

Suddenly, another voice greets Derek ...

"Hello, Derek" greets the voice

Derek looks round to see a familiar face ...

It's Beryl ... who he met a few weeks ago!

"Fancy a dance, love?" asks Beryl (Smiling)

"Yes, I would love to, Beryl" replies Derek (Smiles)

Beryl and Derek take to the dance floor ...

"You see it takes all sorts to make a World" advises Dorothy (member of staff)

"I'm so glad for Derek ... he deserves it after what he's been through" replies Geof (another member of staff)

"Why, what happened?" asks Amanda (Sounds intrigued)

"Derek was a bit of a Mummy's boy ... but not anymore" advises Dorothy (Looks serious)

"There's still life in the old dog yet" mumbles Mike (Laughs)

Time is Tight is now playing indicating the change over from the "live" band to the DJ and records ...

The DJ plays an upbeat mix of modern pop music ...

"Well, Amanda I think it's time we showed these old ones how to boogie" laughs Tim

"Less of the old" replies Dorothy (Laughing)

Dale Watson and his wife, Constance, mingle with their staff ...

The DJ plays "Rhinestone Cowboy" by Glen Campbell

"This brings back memories" advises Dale (Smiling)

"It reminds me of when I worked at a company in Tong" adds Dale

"You were there?" asks Bob (Looks stunned)

"Oh, he was there" advises Constance (Sounds serious)

"Why, what happened?" asks Muriel (Sounds intrigued)

Dale and Constance sit down with Muriel and Bob and several other staff members ...

"Oh, Dale had a fling with someone in Sales" advises Constance

"Really?" replies Muriel (Looks stunned)

"It was before we married, of course" explains Constance

"So, what happened?" asks Muriel (Looks intrigued)

"He fell for a brunette, a girl called Christine" adds Constance

"She was a pretty thing ... couldn't work out her body language though" advises Dale (Sounds stunned)

"So, what happened, Dale ... I mean, Sir?" asks Bob (Smiling)

"Nothing really, Bob ... it was just a bit of an infatuation" explains Dale

"Infatuation my eye" replies Constance (Looks daggers)

"He got several girls hot under the collar" adds Constance

"Why, what happened?" asks Muriel (Sounds stunned)

"Christine left the company" advises Dale (Looks sad)

"I never saw her again ... it's such a long time ago" adds Dale

Meanwhile, Amanda and Tim are grooving with several other staff members on the dance floor ...

The DJ plays a Cliff Richard track ... We don't talk Anymore ...

"I've always loved Cliff" advises Beryl to Derek (Smiling)

"Me too, Beryl" replies Derek (Laughs)

"You know it's funny how we came here before and never spoke to each other" adds Derek

"Yes, I know, Derek ... it must have been fate though" replies Beryl

"Here we are" explains Beryl (Smiling)

"Yea ... here we are" advises Derek (Looks happy)

"Maybe all of this will be the start of something" replies Beryl

"Yea, maybe it will" adds Derek (Sounds serious)

"Watch this space" laughs Beryl and Derek

Bob and Muriel also look back on fond memories ...

"Tonight, reminds me of how we met, Muriel" advises Bob (Smiles)

"I thought we'd agreed not to go down that road, Bob" replies Muriel

"I know ...but" adds Bob (Looks serious)

"Well, we work together and it's turning out for the better" explains Muriel

"What about a second chance, love?" asks Bob (Sounds serious)

"Maybe ... let's see what happens in the future" replies Muriel

Dale and Constance call the staff together ...

"I know this is not the time or the place" advises Dale (Sounds serious)

"For what?" asks Jonathan (Looks concerned)

"Well, you might as well know now" adds Dale (Sounds serious)

"Know what?" asks Bob (Looks serious)

"Watsons is on the verge of being taken over ... we are merging with another company" advises Dale (Looks excited)

"Who?" asks Muriel (Sounds concerned)

"Dawsons Solicitors in Bradford" explains Dale (Sounds serious)

"Yes, we will become Watson Dawson in about three

weeks' time" adds Dale

"Why?" asks Muriel (Sounds serious)

"We need investment to continue our future, Muriel" replies Dale

"What about our jobs?" asks Derek (Looks serious)

"You're all safe ... there will be no redundancies" explains Dale

"Anyway, that's all I can say" adds Dale (Looks serious)

"Have a lovely evening" instructs Dale (Smiling)

Bob, Derek, and Jonathan retire to the bar area ...

"Well, that's put a damper on it" advises Jonathan (Looks serious)

"Well, we all heard Dale say no redundancies" explains Bob (Smiles)

"That's all talk, mate" adds Jonathan (Looks concerned)

"Let's just wait and see" replies Derek (Sounds philosophical)

Back to the dancing ...

The DJ begins to make an announcement ...

"We would like to wish everyone from Watsons Solicitors a very good evening at this their Annual Dance" advises the DJ (Cheers)

"OK ... we're going to have a Limbo contest" adds the DJ

"I need three males and three females" explains the DJ (Smiling)

"Don't all rush to the stage at once" advises the DJ (Laughs)

"Where's Judas?" asks Jonathan (Looks annoyed)

"Who is Judas?" asks Tim (Looks around)

"Dale ... who else?" insists Jonathan (Sounds tipsy)

"Now, now boys ... Dale is only thinking of our long-term future" explains Muriel (Smiles)

"Sorry, Muriel ... yes, I guess he is" adds Jonathan (Smiling)

It's Limbo Contest time ...

The DJ begins to play several reggae tracks ...

First up ... Derek

"How low can you go?" asks the DJ (Smiling)

"Wow, it's Derek" advises Tim (Looks stunned)

"Boy, has he changed" adds Tim (Laughs)

"You see what the love of a good woman can do?" advises Muriel (Laughs)

"Why is Derek in love?" asks Tim (Sounds serious)

"Yes, of course he is ... can't you tell?" explains Muriel

"Who with?" asks Tim (Looks stunned)

"A lady called Beryl ... and I'm glad for him" adds Muriel

"So am I, Muriel ... so am I" replies Tim (Smiling)

Next up, Bob ...

"Oh, this is getting silly now" advises Amanda (Looks fed up)

"What's going on?" asks Muriel (Looks concerned)

"It's Bob" replies Tim (Looks serious)

"Oh, he's had a few too many" advises Jonathan (Looks concerned)

"I think Bob is trying to impress you, Muriel" advises Constance (Smiles)

"He's still got it" replies Muriel (Smiling)

"I'm going to have a go" advises Amanda (Looks serious)

The DJ makes a further announcement ...

"Please keep a hand on your modesty" advises the DJ (Sounds serious)

Amanda's miniskirt leaves nothing to the imagination!

"Where's Dale?" asks Constance (Looks concerned)

"He's talking to Keith, the General Manager" explains Dorothy (Points)

"So, he's not committed harry carry then?" laughs Jonathan

"He's not getting up to his old tricks, is he?" asks Derek (Laughs)

"I'd better go and find him" replies Constance (Smirks)

The DJ announces the winner of the Limbo Contest ...

"... and the winner is" advises the DJ (Smiles)

"Drum roll, please" adds the DJ

"Bob" replies the DJ (All Cheering)

Bob is flabbergasted!

Muriel decides to get up on stage and kisses Bob on the lips ...

"Presentation time" explains the DJ (Shakes hands with Bob)

Bob is presented with a trophy for being the winner!

Muriel whispers in Bob's ear ...

"OK, I'm willing to give it another go, if you are" explains Muriel

"Really?" replies Bob (Looks happy)

"We have to stick to the rules though" advises Muriel (Sounds serious)

"OK ... it's a deal and don't worry I won't put a foot wrong" laughs Bob (Kisses Muriel)

The DJ starts to play Party Anthems ...

It really is PARTY TIME!!!

The mood and atmosphere of the occasion has really changed ...

Watsons staff are all on the dance floor ...

The DJ asks for everyone to be in a ring and begins to play ...

GERRYCULLEN

YOU'LL NEVER WALK ALONE

What a night ... a night to remember!

DISCOTHEQUE

It's back to the Seventies and Eighties for this six-part comedy themed drama series of stories set against the backdrop of disco music and styles of fashion in a very modern World!

Richard and Gerry discover a vastly different scene to that of the Swinging Sixties!

They take in all the disco venues in Leeds and Bradford and find girls have changed so much in style to those of the Swinging Sixties.

Way out fashions, twenty-four-inch flares, hot pants, platform shoes, kipper ties, The Persuaders, Charlies Angels, the Fiesta, Sheffield, Cinderella's, and Tiffany's in Leeds are all part of it!

The Nouveau is a particular favourite, as is Len's Bar, Digby's, and Parkers Wine Bar!

How will Richard and Gerry progress in this disco era?

THESE ARE ... THE
GOOD TIMES!

AM I IN LOVE ... OR WHAT?

Richard and Gerry agree to meet again in the bar area of the Crowne Plaza Hotel in Leeds and discuss their memories of the Seventies and Eighties in detail ...

It's not long before they begin to reminisce about when they used to go to discotheques in Leeds and Bradford ...

PRESENT DAY ...

"Do you remember when we used to go to discos back in the Seventies, Rich?" asks Gerry (Deep in thought)

"Yes ... very well" replies Richard

"The music was electrifying ... and the girls" adds Richard (Smiles)

"Oh, especially the girls" replies Gerry (Laughs)

"Back in 1974 I worked for a company in Tong" advises Gerry

"I used to know a girl called Christine" adds Gerry

"Did you become attached?" asks Richard (Looks intrigued)

"We would walk down for the bus together ... nice girl, Christine" remembers Gerry

"What happened to her?" asks Richard (Looks serious)

"I really don't know ... the last time I saw her was in Summer 1975" explains Gerry

"Wow, that's 50 years ago" replies Richard (Sounds serious)

"What else can you remember from back then?" asks Richard

"I remember a company night out to the Fiesta in Sheffield" replies Gerry (Sounds sincere)

"The Fiesta?" asks Richard (Looks puzzled)

The Fiesta was a cabaret style night club situated on Arundel Gate in Sheffield. Many celebrities of the Sixties and Seventies performed there.

"What happened to the Fiesta?" adds Richard (Looks intrigued)

"The Fiesta was booming in the Seventies, but it closed permanently in 1980" explains Gerry (Looks sad)

"Why what happened, Gerry?" asks Richard (Looks concerned)

"Sheffield was a city with a booming economy and high employment but by the Eighties the steel and coal industries went into steep decline" advises Gerry

(Looks sad)

"So, what happened on your company night out?" asks Richard

"How can you remember so long ago?" adds Richard (Sounds puzzled)

"Since I was in my coma at Leeds General Infirmary in March 2018 everything has been advanced ... I can remember everything so clearly" replies Gerry

"It's as if you've got a photographic memory" adds Richard

BACK TO 1974 ...

A coach came to pick up everyone from our works in Tong ...

"You look lovely, tonight ... Christine" advises Gerry (Smiles)

"Thank you ... you don't look too bad yourself" replies Christine (Smiling)

"Are we going to have a dance at the Fiesta?" asks Gerry

"What do you think?" replies Christine (Winks)

Everyone gets on to the coach and after the driver counts everyone on board, he drives off down the M1 towards Sheffield ...

"Hey, you're in there" advises Brian (Smiles)

"Christine's just a friend ... nothing else, Brian" replies

Gerry (Smiling)

"That's what they all say" laughs Brian

"Hey, you can have a dance with me young man" advises Sally (Winks)

"Your top of the list, love" replies Gerry (Smiling)

"Don't forget" adds Sally (Laughs)

"Don't worry Sally I won't love" advises Gerry (Winks)

After an hour's drive the coach eventually arrives outside the Fiesta in Sheffield ...

The main act, Mike Read (Comedian) is due on stage around 10pm.

Before that it's disco all the way!

Girls are dancing in cages to the beat at either side of the stage!

"Wow, I've never seen that before, Brian" advises Gerry (Looks stunned)

"Oh, it's all the rage in London, mate" replies Brian (Smiles)

The DJ plays a selection of upbeat disco pop records ...

"Come on, Brian ... let's join Christine and the other girls" advises Gerry

"OK ... let's go for it" replies Brian (Laughs)

"You took your time, love" advises Christine (Smiling)

"Have you been waiting for me, Christine?" asks Gerry (Looks stunned)

"Yes, love, of course who else?" adds Christine (Winks)

"They will begin to talk about us, Christine" explains Gerry (Sounds concerned)

"Well, are you bothered, Gerry?" asks Christine (Smiling)

"No ... I'm not if you're not, Christine" advises Gerry

PRESENT DAY

"It sounds like you had a good time at the Fiesta" advises Richard

"Yes, I did" replies Gerry (Smiling)

"So, what happened between you and Christine?" asks Richard (Looks intrigued)

"Christine and I remained good friends ... but that's all that happened" explains Gerry

"Why didn't you take it further?" asks Richard (Looks baffled)

"Oh, I always remembered the don't mix business with pleasure rule" adds Gerry

"I also thought she wasn't in my league" explains Gerry

"But now you'll never know ... because you didn't ask" replies Richard

"Yes, in hindsight maybe I should have taken it further" explains Gerry

"The story of my life ... but I fondly remember, Christine" adds Gerry

"So, what happened to her?" asks Richard

"I genuinely don't really know what happened to Christine" advises Gerry

"She just seemed to disappear off the globe" adds Gerry

"Hey, Rich ... what about the time when we were at the old Bradford Mecca in 1974 and met those two girls from Thornton?" asks Gerry

"I can't remember them ... you'll have to remind me" replies Richard

"Rebecca, do you remember her?" adds Gerry

Rebecca was five foot four, had long wavy hair, attractive. She was wearing a cream blouse with a mini skirt ... and with her friend, Clare.

"Sorry, I still can't remember" advises Richard (Looks puzzled)

"Oh, we started getting very daring in those days" replies Gerry

"You were home from university at the time" explains Gerry

BACK TO 1974 ...

Richard and Gerry in conversation ...

"Why don't we go to Bradford Mecca, tonight, Rich?"

asks Gerry

"Yea, good idea ... why not?" replies Richard

Gerry and Richard arrive at the Mecca Locarno on Manningham Lane in Bradford ...

They both check themselves in the vast array of mirrors in the Stag Room and then enter the huge ballroom ... both looking very cool!

Gerry is wearing his baby blue twenty-four-inch flares, an open necked shirt and a typical Seventies jacket designed by Jonathan Silver ...

"Where did you get the jacket?" asks Richard (Looks in approval)

"Oh, from Jonathan Silver's shop inside of Kirkgate Market" replies Gerry

"Do you like my gear, Rich?" adds Gerry (Smiles)

"Oh, it looks really good" replies Richard (Smiling)

The dance floor is now starting to fill with lots of girls dancing around their handbags!

"OK... it's time to be the persuaders ... lets go on to the dance floor, Rich" instructs Gerry (Smiling)

"Ask the usual questions" advises Richard (Smiles)

Gerry and Richard decide to ask a couple of girls for a dance ...

"Can we have this dance?" asks Gerry (Smiling)

"Sure" replies one of the girls (Big Smile)

"Hi, I'm Richard ... this is Gerry" greets Richard

(Smiles)

"Hi, I'm Clare ... she's Rebecca" replies Clare (Smiling)

"Hello Rebecca ... nice to meet you" greets Gerry

All the usual questions are asked ...

"Do you come here often?" asks Gerry (Smiling)

Rebecca nods, smiles and continues to dance ...

PRESENT DAY

"How did we get on, Gerry?" asks Richard (Sounds serious)

"Oh, you had a good time with Clare" replies Gerry (Smiles)

"... and you?" asks Richard

"I got on like a house on fire with Rebecca" advises Gerry

"So, what happened ... did you make a date with her?" adds Richard (Sounds inquisitive)

"Yea, we had a few dates ... and I met her brothers and sisters" explains Gerry

"Then what?" asks Richard (Looks stunned)

"She joined the NHS as a student nurse in early 1975" adds Gerry

"What happened then?" adds Richard (Sounds intrigued)

"I guess that was it" replies Gerry

"I never really saw her again" advises Gerry

"Both she and I moved on" replies Gerry (Sighs)

"I did bump into her again though at the old Mecca, Rich" explains Gerry

"What happened then?" asks Richard

"Oh, we were polite to each other ... but that was it" adds Gerry

"A case of Deja vu?" adds Richard (Sounds philosophical)

"Yes ... Deja vu" replies Gerry

"We were both young at the time... and our lives were ahead of us" explains Gerry

"So, you never saw Rebecca again?" asks Richard

"No ... that was the end of that as they say" replies Gerry (Laughs)

"Any more conquests?" asks Richard (Looks serious)

"Well, I remember one in July 1975 ... it was midsummer, again at the Bradford Mecca ...

Summertime City by Mike Batt was playing ...

"Excuse me ... do you mind if I have this dance?" asks Gerry

"Not at all" replies a young woman (Smiles)

"I'm Gerry ... that is Jimmy" advises Gerry (Smiling)

"Who was Jimmy?" asks Richard (Looks puzzled)

"Rebecca's brother" explains Gerry (Laughs)

"What did he think of your breakup with Rebecca?" asks Richard

"Nothing really ... we were all young back then" replies Gerry

"Anyway, we met two girls from Guiseley" recalls Gerry

"What happened?" asks Richard

"I took Diana out" advises Gerry (Smiles)

"I went to meet her at her house" adds Gerry

"What happened next?" adds Richard

"I was met by her dad" explains Gerry (Looks annoyed)

"He said ... who are you?" replies Gerry

"I said ... who are you?" laughs Gerry

"Anyway, that's the end of that story" adds Gerry

"I decided to nip that one in the bud" explains Gerry

"There's as good as fish in the sea ... that ever came out of it" quips Gerry

"You said it mate" laughs Richard

MAN ABOUT TOWN

It's now 1976 ... Gerry goes his own way while Richard is now at University in London.

Everything is still very much alive on the disco scene in Leeds and Bradford!

PRESENT DAY

"Well, what did you get up to in 1976?" asks Richard (Sounds intrigued)

"I remember buying my first car in May" remembers Gerry

"What kind of car was it?" asks Richard

"It was a Vauxhall Firenza ... and it was a rust bucket" laughs Gerry

"Come to think of it, I do remember it" replies Richard (Laughs)

"Didn't the gear stick come off when you drove it?" adds Richard

"Yes, that's the one, mate ... it was a real eye opener" laughs Gerry

"So, what happened in 1976?" asks Richard

"OK, I'll tell you" replies Gerry (Smiles)

BACK TO 1976 ...

"I always wanted to see Elton John in concert, and I did" replies Gerry

"How did you manage to get tickets?" asks Richard (Looks intrigued)

"Oh, I had to join his fan club to get them" replies Gerry (Laughs)

"And I could have made a fortune if I had sold them on the night" explains Gerry

"Where was the concert?" asks Richard

"It was at Leeds Grand Theatre ... and it was a complete sell out" advises Gerry

"What happened after that?" asks Richard (Looks intrigued)

"I started going into Leeds on a Thursday night, and I decided I would try the New Venture Singles dance in the Banqueting Suite in the Merrion Centre" replies Gerry (Smiles)

"How did you get on there?" asks Richard

"Oh, very well ... I also met another character there ... Ernest" adds Gerry

"We remained friends for a while but he kind of went a bit funny" explains Gerry (Looks serious)

"Funny in what way?" asks Richard (Looks serious)

"I presume not as in ha ha" laughs Richard

"No ... for example, when he pulled a woman ... I was no longer visible ... do you know what I mean, Rich?" asks Gerry

"Oh, yes I think I get the picture" replies Richard

"He would come out with various laugh lines" adds Gerry

"What kind of laugh lines?" asks Richard

"He used to say ... If I were you love, I would talk to anyone that would talk to me" replies Gerry

"He really was funny" adds Gerry

"Do you remember, Summer 76 when it was really hot?" asks Gerry

"Oh, yea I remember ... it went on and on" replies Richard

"Someone told me about a new nightclub on Eastgate in Leeds called the Nouveau" advises Gerry

"Oh, I remember the Nouveau" replies Richard (Looks in thought)

"Remember it was quite classy ... no rough types in there" explains Gerry

"Didn't we go there?" asks Richard (Tries to remember)

"Yes, of course we did" replies Gerry (Smiles)

"It was quite a plush place ... and very refined ... you know what I mean" adds Gerry

"So, what happened?" asks Richard (Looks serious)

"Remember when I went over to the bar to order our drinks?" advises Gerry

"Well, I noticed this very slim kid at the bar asking where the restaurant was and his table" adds Gerry

"Did you know him?" asks Steve (Sounds intrigued)

"Wait for it ... he had long dark hair, a grey jeans jacket, black trousers and an open necked shirt" replies Gerry

"I really only saw him from behind" explains Gerry

"Well, who was it?" asks Richard (Sounds intrigued)

"It was Cliff" advises Gerry (Smiling)

"Cliff who?" replies Richard (Looks surprised)

"Cliff Richard ... he had just done a gig at the Grand Theatre" explains Gerry

"I asked the DJ to play Devil Woman ... and he did" explains Gerry

"Did it provoke any reaction?" asks Richard (Looks serious)

"Oh yes, it did ... Cliff was in conversation with his managers but looked very happy ... probably at the thought that the DJ was playing his song" laughs Gerry

"Did anyone go to talk to him?" asks Richard (Looks

intrigued)

"No ... neither did I ... and I'm sure all he wanted was his privacy" adds Gerry

"Any other tales of meeting famous people?" asks Richard

"I did bump into Frankie Howerd once near the dark arches on his way to the Dragonara hotel" explains Gerry

"The Dragonara ... it's now the Hilton" advises Richard

"Yes, that's it ... your right it is now the Hilton" replies Gerry

"Did he say anything?" asks Richard

"No ... he was a bit creepy ... I just walked past quickly" replies Gerry

"I had my twenty-four-inch flares on ... open necked shirt ... boy I was a Seventies man about town then" laughs Gerry

BACK TO THE PRESENT DAY

"Hey, do you remember when we saw THE THREE DEGREES at Batley Variety Club?" asks Richard (Smiles)

"Yea, I remember ... now they were a class act" replies Gerry

"Happy days" adds Richard (Laughing)

"Very happy days, mate" laughs Gerry

"Do you remember when we saw Gary Glitter?" asks Richard

"Oh, I remember it was a packed house" adds Gerry

"That was way before any scandal came out about him" advises Gerry

"It's a shame Batley Variety Club closed ... it would still have been welcomed by everyone today" adds Richard

"Yea, it was very much of its time and it's sad that it's gone" replies Gerry

"I may write something about the Variety Club in another book" explains Gerry

"When?" asks Richard (Sounds intrigued)

"Let's just say that it may be in the near future" explains Gerry

IT MECCA ME SICK!

It's 1979 and times are a changing ... Donna Summer is the Queen of Pop, and the Bee Gees are up there with them all!

Richard and Gerry have another reunion at the Crowne Plaza hotel in Leeds where they carry on their ... THIS IS YOUR LIFE STORY!

PRESENT DAY

"Shouldn't that be this is our life?" asks Richard (Smiles)

"Yes, your right mate, this is our life" replies Gerry (Smiling)

BACK TO 1979 ...

Richard and Gerry meet up for a rare evening out in July at the old Mecca Locarno ballroom on Manningham Lane in Bradford.

"Come on, let's dance with those two over there" advises Richard

"OK, let's go" replies Gerry (Smiling)

"Be brave ... just go to the next two if nothing happens" adds Gerry

Richard and Gerry's luck is in ...

"Hi ... can we have this dance?" asks Richard (Smiles)

That was met with no response!

"We're dancing anyway ... who cares" advises Gerry

PRESENT DAY

"What happened?" asks Richard (Looks intrigued)

"Don't you remember?" laughs Gerry

"No ... I'm afraid I don't" adds Richard (Tries to remember)

"Yours was OK ... mine was deaf and dumb" replies Gerry

"Really?" replies Richard (Looks stunned)

"Yea" adds Gerry

"What did we do?" asks Richard (Looks surprised)

"We made a quick exit ... stage left" replies Gerry

The DJ started to play Tragedy by the Bee Gees ...

"Well, that's an omen" advises Richard (Smiling)

"It really was a tragedy back then, Rich" laughs Gerry

"Never mind ... plenty more fish in the sea" quips Richard

"What happened after that?" asks Richard (Looks inquisitive)

"We met two more girls on the dance floor" advises Gerry

"Boy, we were both sex gods back then, Rich" laughs Gerry

"That's a joke" adds Gerry (Both laughing)

"What else happened in 1979?" asks Richard (Sounds intrigued)

"I continued to have nights out at the Mecca Locarno in Bradford ... the music was just brilliant then" advises Gerry (Smiles)

"How did you get on?" asks Richard (Looks surprised)

"Well, I remember going back to Tiffany's in Leeds with old Ernest" replies Gerry (Laughs)

"What happened there?" asks Richard

"There was a stunning blonde on the door as we entered the Foyer" replies Gerry

"Ernest charmed the pants off her and got her phone number" explains Gerry (Smiling)

"Why don't you give me your phone number ... call me if you want a night out" advises the young woman (Smiles)

"It was as easy as that?" asks Richard (Looks stunned)

"Yes ... and it worked" replies Gerry (Smiling)

"She said ... OK, I will remember" adds Gerry (Laughs)

Then she said to me ...

"Aren't you going to give me your phone number too?" advises Gerry

"What did you do?" asks Richard (Sounds stunned)

"I said, sure here is my phone number" replies Gerry (Smiling)

"I think she was called Stephanie" advises Gerry (Thinks back)

"Anyway ... a few days later" adds Gerry

"Don't tell me ... you got the call?" asks Richard (Smiles)

"Actually, no I didn't ... but Ernest did" laughs Gerry

"What happened then?" adds Richard (Sounds intrigued)

"I met Stephanie again on the way into Tiffany's in the Merrion Centre a couple of weeks later" explains Gerry

"What did she say?" asks Richard (Looks concerned)

"She said ... I tried to call you last week ... and I got this weird guy on the end of the phone and couldn't get rid of him" laughs Gerry

"I said that was Ernest" advises Gerry (Both laughing)

"Did you take her out?" asks Richard

"We arranged to meet but something else came up" laughs Gerry

"That's the story of my life, mate" laughs Richard

"Mine too" adds Gerry (Both Laughing)

"What else happened in 1979?" asks Richard

"Well, I remember going to the Griffin Hotel and Wellesley Hotel in Leeds and the hotel near Foster Square in Bradford" remembers Gerry

"Why what happened there?" asks Richard (Looks intrigued)

"I met some nice people there while you were at University" explains Gerry

"Someone told me about the Old Mill Ballroom in Wetherby on Saturday nights ... and Sundays at the Griffin" advises Gerry (Smiling)

"I met Jack there at the New Venture Singles in the Merrion Centre" adds Gerry (Smiles)

"He always told the girls to look after me" laughs Gerry

"And did they?" asks Richard (Sounds intrigued)

"Yes, they always did" adds Gerry (Laughs)

"Jack was a lovely man ... he was like my dad" laughs Gerry

"I think Jack lived in Wetherby" explains Gerry

"Did you take his advice?" asks Richard (Looks serious)

"Yes, I did ... and I decided to go to the Old Mill as he suggested the following Saturday" replies Gerry (Smiling)

The Old Mill Ballroom was old fashioned, and it looked

as if it was in a time warp. You could walk all the way round it.

The owners arrived by barge on a Saturday and only opened it on that day.

"What happened?" asks Richard (Sounds intrigued)

"They had a live band, and the owner played a mismatch of records ... he used to get his knickers in a twist" laughs Gerry

"The records he used to play were appalling ... the only decent one he played was at the beginning (every week) it was by Fern Kinney" adds Gerry (Smiles)

"Now every time I hear Together, we are Beautiful it reminds me of way back then" laughs Gerry

"I always remember what Ernest used to say" adds Gerry

"What was that?" asks Richard (Looks serious)

"Oh, he used to say ... remember if you haven't pulled by midnight there is always another day" laughs Gerry

"Was he right?" asks Richard

"Yes, I think he was ... anyway it was carefree back then" remembers Gerry

"It was a lovely place to go on a Saturday night though" advises Gerry

"I particularly remember the lovely run in the car through the countryside, through Leeds and on to Wetherby" adds Gerry

"What ever happened to Alex?" asks Gerry (Looks serious)

"Alex from Harrogate?" replies Richard (Tries to remember)

"Yes, that's him" advises Gerry (Looks intrigued)

"I don't know" explains Richard

"I always remember when he used to come to Bradford Mecca, and he coined the phrase ... it mecca me sick" laughs Gerry

"What you probably don't know is that Alex worked for a company in Tong in the early Seventies" explains Gerry

"How do you know that?" asks Richard (Looks stunned)

"I remember as I worked for their sister company, at the same site" advises Gerry

"I kept going to the old Mecca Locarno in Manningham Lane until it's closure in 1988" adds Gerry

"So sad" replies Richard (Looks concerned)

"Yes, it was ... it was the end of an era" replies Gerry (Smiles)

"It was ... we had so many wonderful times and memories there" adds Gerry

"It set me on the course for more wonderful things" explains Gerry

"My future seemed to open up before me in 1987 ... and it took on another dimension" adds Gerry (Smiles)

BRINGING ON THE GOOD TIMES

The link period 1981 – 1987 ... Tiffany's, Len's Bar, Digby's, and Parker's Wine Bar in Leeds ... going somewhere, but going nowhere?

PRESENT DAY

Another meeting at the Crowne Plaza Hotel in Leeds ...

Richard and Gerry meet again in the relaxing reception area close to the bar ...

More candid memories of a period well remembered in time ...

"Did you ever go to Parker's Wine Bar when you worked in Leeds, Rich?" asks Gerry

"No, I can't say I ever did ... what about you?" replies Richard

"Oh, first time I went there Elton's Song for Guy was playing ... it was a popular venue then" advises Gerry (Smiling)

"What about anything else?" asks Richard

"I remember going to Len's Bar and Digby's in particular" replies Gerry

BACK TO 1985 ...

Ernest and Gerry meet up with a couple of ladies we met at the Merrion Banqueting suite the night before ...

Jane and Becky ...

"Now, nothing wrong with that" advises Richard (Laughs)

"Well, what happened?" adds Richard (Looks intrigued)

"We were all just talking at a table for four, then something quite unusual happened" replies Gerry

"A girl came over to me and asked me for a dance" advises Gerry (Looks stunned)

"She was very pretty, had long dark hair and was quite attractive" explains Gerry (Sounds serious)

"What did you do?" asks Richard (Sounds stunned)

"I said, sorry love ... I'm with someone" replies Gerry

"That'll never happen again" laughs Richard

"Too right ... it never did, Rich" laughs Gerry

"A case of Deja vu" adds Richard

"Yea ... a massive case of Deja vu" replies Gerry

(Smiles)

"Well, it was a moment never to be forgotten" laughs Gerry

"How did your dates go?" asks Richard

"It was just another date ... but Ernest was another thing" adds Gerry

"Why, what happened with Ernest?" adds Richard (Looks intrigued)

"Oh, Ernest met up with Jane again at her home" explains Gerry

"He said she had a little son, and he was quite a handful" adds Gerry

"Ernest said the son got hold of her gold wristwatch and dropped it on the fireplace on purpose and it smashed to bits" advises Gerry (Sounds serious)

"Well, kids will be kids" adds Richard (Laughs)

"Yea, but old Ernest had other ideas" explains Gerry

"Oh?" replies Richard (Looks puzzled)

"Ernest told him not to do it" adds Gerry

"You know what happened, then" explains Gerry

"The little son dropped it and laughed" adds Gerry

"This incensed Ernest ... and he promptly gave him a clip around the ear" advises Gerry

"You can't do that these days" replies Richard (Looks mortified)

"No, you can't ... but it happened in 1985" adds Gerry

Digby's was a kind of plush place, and the DJ played good music ... it was very sophisticated and attracted certain types of people!

"Tell me about the Wellesley Hotel" asks Richard (Sounds intrigued)

"Oh, the New Venture group tried this venue after the Merrion Banqueting Suite" replies Gerry

"Was it still a plush venue?" adds Richard

"Yes, it had an upstairs ballroom which doubled up as a meeting room" explains Gerry

"The Singles dance was on a Thursday evening just as it was in the Banqueting Suite" recalls Gerry

"Did you pull there?" asks Richard (Looks serious)

"Not really ... it was more of a night out than anything else" explains Gerry

"What about the Griffin Hotel on Sundays?" adds Richard

"Now that was the place to be ... it was always packed" advises Gerry

"Did you have fun there?" replies Richard

"I always remember this slim spectacle wearing girl" explains Gerry

"She looked as though she was wearing everything out from the inside when she danced" laughs Gerry

"She will be on her Zimmer now" laughs Richard

"You could be right there, Rich" adds Gerry (Both laughing)

"Well, you certainly brought on the good times when you were out" adds Richard

"Oh, yes it was a wonderful social scene, at the time" replies Gerry

"But?" asks Richard (Sounds puzzled)

"Well, it felt like something was missing" advises Gerry

"Missing?" replies Richard (Looks intrigued)

"Yea ... you know a certain spark ... and it all felt like a merry go round ... you remember the scene ... I needed something more" explains Gerry

"More?" asks Richard (Looks stunned)

"Yes ... there's more to life" adds Gerry (Looks serious)

"... and I found it when I joined Zodiac in September 1987" advises Gerry (Smiles)

"I wasn't sure at first, but it turned out to be the making of me" explains Gerry (Smiling)

"I will tell you more about that at our next meeting" adds Gerry

"Did you still go to the old Bradford Mecca?" asks Richard

"Oh yea, right up until it's closure" explains Gerry

"Good times ... that's where it all began for me" quips Gerry

"Yea, me too ... gone are the days of the Bobby Brook Band and the revolving stage revealing the DJ playing records" adds Richard

"Whatever happened to it?" asks Richard (Looks intrigued)

"Someone else took it over, renamed it, but it was the end for me" explains Gerry (Looks sad)

"What about Cinderella's here in Leeds?" asks Richard

"Oh, Cinders was the place to be, and it was then owned by Peter Stringfellow" advises Gerry

"But Peter eventually sold it to Mecca ... now they never mentioned that but eventually it bombed" advises Gerry

"It had had it's day" asks Richard

"Yes, in Leeds it did ... it was a shame because it was the place to be ... but times were changing" adds Gerry

"Not for the better" advises Richard

"No, you're absolutely right about that, Rich, not for the better" replies Gerry

"The good times were coming to an end ... punk was taking over" adds Gerry

"What did you do?" asks Richard (Looks intrigued)

"Oh ... Digby's and the Old Mill at Wetherby were still in operation, so I used to go to those places and Tiffany's" explains Gerry

"What about the Merrion Banqueting Suite, next

door?" adds Richard

"The New Venture on a Thursday night eventually closed due to a decline in numbers" explains Gerry

"I did go to the Bali Hai a few times" remembers Gerry

"The Bali Hai?" asks Richard

"Yes, it was part of Tiffany's, except it was separate ... and it had a very good Polynesian type of atmosphere though" adds Gerry

"What about the music?" asks Richard

"They played lots of Soul and pop music, Rich" advises Gerry

"When the disco scene started to change it was all over" explains Gerry

"What did you do?" asks Richard

"I started to look for other options ... and found them in a big way in 1987" laughs Gerry

ZODIAC/MIRAGE

September 1987 was an excessively substantial change for Gerry!

With the decline of the disco scene, Gerry opted to join Zodiac, a national Singles social scene based at Tapas Bar in Lower Briggate, Leeds.

Gerry arranges to meet Richard for another nostalgic trip down memory lane at the Crowne Plaza in Leeds.

Gerry remembers just how it was over 30 years ago, and of his plans for an Event in the future!

Richard and Gerry order at the bar then find a secluded table to continue their conversation about the past ...

"So, tell me about your time at Zodiac and Mirage, Gerry" asks Richard (Sounds intrigued)

"Oh, you would have loved them both, Rich" replies Gerry (Smiling)

"Why, and in what way?" adds Richard (Looks intrigued)

"I had so many good times there" replies Gerry (Smiles)

"And there were so many women ... we were fighting them off" explains Gerry (Laughs)

"That's a joke, right?" laughs Richard

"Maybe" adds Gerry (Winks)

"Yes, it really was a great time in my life, Rich" advises Gerry

"I loved being a member of both Zodiac and Mirage ... they were the making of me" adds Gerry

"How do you mean?" asks Richard (Sounds intrigued)

"Well, everything changed for me when I joined" explains Gerry

BACK TO 1987 ...

"I had seen an advertisement in the Yorkshire Evening Post, and it sort of sold it to me, there and then" advises Gerry (Smiling)

"So, what happened next?" adds Richard (Smiles)

"I phoned for details ... and this is what happened" explains Gerry

"Hello, I'm David" replies a voice

"Hi, David ... I'm calling about becoming a member of Zodiac" advises Gerry

"OK ... we have a following nationwide and we are well represented in the West Yorkshire area" explains David

"In fact, we have a meeting tomorrow at Tapas in Leeds" adds David

"Are you interested, Gerry?" asks David

"Yes, I'd like to join, David" enthuses Gerry (Smiling)

"It costs £90 a year ... are you still interested?" adds David

"Yes, absolutely" replies Gerry

"OK send in three cheques ... one dated today for £30 and the other two at monthly intervals" explains David

"The reason we make a charge is to restrict certain individuals from our Events and Bar Nights" adds David

"It sounds just what I'm looking for, David" replies Gerry

"OK ... you send off your cheques today to this address" advises David

"I will send out all the information you need plus your red membership card and Zodiac monthly magazine ... and remember we are a national singles organization ... so you can go anywhere" enthuses David

"OK ... I will be in Tapas from 8pm tomorrow" advises David

"I will look forward to seeing you then and I will introduce you to Mike and lots of other members" adds David

"Well, go on what happened next?" asks Richard (Looks intrigued)

"I met David at Tapas as arranged ... after that it was just amazing" replies Gerry

"Where was Tapas?" asks Richard (Sounds intrigued)

"Tapas was situated under the iron bridge in Lower Briggate" explains Gerry

"What was it like inside?" asks Richard (Sounds interested)

"It had a reception area then you entered through another door ... the bar was in front of you ... it had a DJ and dance floor to the left, and tables, chairs and a standing area to the right" advises Gerry

"I also met another character called Mike" adds Gerry (Smiles)

"Hi, I'm Mike ... Meeter and Greeter here at Tapas" replies Mike (Both shake hands)

"David's told me it's your first night" advises Mike (Smiles)

"Hi, I'm Gerry ... yes, it is Mike" replies Gerry (Smiling)

"OK, check out our notice board of events to the right of the bar" advises Mike (Pointing)

"If you like the sound of anything let me know" adds Mike (Smiles)

"Grab yourself a beer then come back here, and I will introduce you to one or two members" advises Mike

EVERLASTING LOVE

"Well, did you?" asks Richard (Sounds intrigued)

"Yes, I did ... someone was having a Halloween Party in Knaresborough at the weekend" explains Gerry

"Did you go?" asks Richard (Looks serious)

"I sure did ... and it was the start of everything" replies Gerry

"What happened at the party?" asks Richard

"It was fancy dress ... a lot of people had amazing costumes" adds Gerry

"What about you?" asks Richard (Looks intrigued)

"I was casually dressed ... there were lots of ladies too" laughs Gerry

"Did you meet anyone in particular?" asks Richard

"Yes, I met two stunners from York" replies Gerry (Smiling)

"Hi, I'm Jane ... this is Lucy ... we're from York" advises Jane (Smiles)

"Hi, Jane and Lucy ... I'm Gerry from Leeds" advises Gerry (Smiling)

"Oh, we go to Leeds Bar Night quite often ... I hope we see you there next time" adds Jane

"You can count on it, love" replies Gerry (Smiles)

The party starts to get into full swing and the music is ramped up ...

"Come on, darling ... time for a dance" advises Jane (Smiling)

"I don't mind if I do" adds Gerry (Smiles)

"It was as easy as that?" asks Richard (Looks surprised)

"Yes ... it was as easy as that" replies Gerry (Laughs)

"... and she asked you too" quips Richard (Looks stunned)

"I know it was sheer magnetism and they had terrific taste, obviously" laughs Gerry

"Obviously" laughs Richard

"I also met Nick from York there too" advises Gerry

"Nick?" asks Richard (Looks interested)

"Oh, he was the Meeter and Greeter at York" explains Gerry

"Hi, I'm Nick" greets Nick (Both shake hands)

"I see Jane is looking after you?" laughs Nick

"Hi, Nick ... I'm Gerry" (Smiling)

"Yes, and Lucy too" adds Gerry

"Is it your first night?" asks Nick (Smiles)

"Yes, first party" replies Gerry (Smiling)

"Look after him girls" advises Nick

"We will, darling ... we will" replies Jane

"Don't worry, he is in safe hands" replies Jane (Winks)

"The music is a bit funny, Jane" advises Gerry

"What do you mean, darling?" asks Jane (Sounds

EVERLASTING LOVE

puzzled)

"It's a bit flat" replies Gerry (Smiles)

"I've got a tape with me that's more appropriate for dancing to" adds Gerry (Produces tape out of pocket)

"Well, put it on, darling ... let's begin to groove" adds Jane

The mood of the evening and party immediately changes ...

"Whoever put that tape on ... good on you" advises Nick

Gerry laughs at Nick's remarks and nods ...

"I like your moves, Jane" laughs Gerry

"You're a real smooth talker" replies Jane (Smiling)

"You were in there" advises Richard (Looks stunned)

"Oh, Jane was always like that she was a born flirt" explains Gerry

"But yes, she was always on the radar" laughs Gerry

"Everything suddenly went into overdrive" adds Gerry

"Overdrive?" asks Richard (Sounds puzzled)

"I was given a good piece of advice by Mike" replies Gerry

"What was it?" asks Richard (Looks puzzled)

"Oh, to be discreet and also not to let everyone know my business" explains Gerry

"Why?" asks Richard (Sounds stunned)

"Mike said they all talk here" adds Gerry

"So, it really was sound advice?" asks Richard

"Yes, it was ... and I was then bound by it" replies Gerry

"Why?" asks Richard

"Oh, a member called Sue ... she was a pretty thing ... went out with someone called Adam" advises Gerry

"What happened?" asks Richard (Looks intrigued)

"It turned out that he was married ... and it became the talk of Zodiac" replies Gerry

"I see what you mean" adds Richard (Sounds shocked)

"They were right to be discreet" replies Gerry

"It was the beginning of everything for me" adds Gerry

"What do you mean?" asks Richard (Looks intrigued)

"Well, I really enjoyed myself at Zodiac ... but it didn't take off until February 1990 when I also joined another Singles club called Mirage" explains Gerry (Looks serious)

"Why were you a member of two Single clubs?" asks Richard

"Well, Zodiac had Bar nights at Tapas on Tuesday evenings and Mirage had theirs at Jacomelli's in Leeds on Thursday evenings ... both had events on at weekends too" adds Gerry

"Yea, but I still don't understand why join two Singles

clubs?" adds Richard (Looks stunned)

"Well, I thought if one of the clubs had nothing on the other one would, and vice versa" explains Gerry

"Oh, I get your way of thinking now" replies Richard (Smiles)

"So, what happened at Mirage?" asks Richard

FIRST NIGHT AT MIRAGE ...

Gerry walks into Jacomelli's in the Centre of Leeds on a Thursday evening.

He is greeted by Jan the treasurer and founder of the Club.

Gerry decides to join Mirage on the spot and pays his first instalment to Jan. This is a similar set up to Zodiac ...

Surprise, surprise ... Jan was a former member of Zodiac and decided to open her own Singles Club in Leeds ...

"OK, here's your card" advises Jan (Smiles)

Jan is in her late forties, has brown curly hair, wears spectacles, but extremely attractive!

"Have a look at our events board and mingle" adds Jan (Smiles)

It's not long before Gerry is talking to other new members and taken by surprise when he is asked a certain question ...

"Hi, I'm Terri ... will you put on a do for us?" asks Terri

(Smiling)

Terri is a tall brunette, has green eyes, and incredibly attractive ...

"Well, I don't know ... I have never given one before, Terri" replies Gerry (Looks gob smacked)

"Don't worry ... you can put it on at the Green Community Centre in the centre of Horsforth ... we have all our parties there" explains Terri (Big Smile)

Gerry is cornered and feels as though he has been put on the spot!

After a lot of persuasion from Terri he decides to give it a go ...

"OK, Terri ... I'll do it" advises Gerry (Looks stunned)

"When?" asks Terri (Looks serious)

"Let's say in two- or three-weeks' time on a Saturday night" adds Gerry

"Super ... have you got any idea what you will do?" asks Terri

Gerry looks stunned ...

"I'll let you know next week, Terri" replies Gerry (Looks anxious)

"OK, love ... are you coming to our disco with Dave on Saturday?" asks Terri (Smiling)

"Yes, I am" replies Gerry (Smiles)

"See you there, love" adds Terri (Big Smile)

"We can have a few dances" explains Terri (Winks)

"Count on it, Terri" laughs Gerry (Smiling)

Saturday arrives and Gerry walks into the Green Community Centre in Horsforth ...

The disco dance is being staged on the first floor with Dave on his double tape decks!

"Wow, Dave ... I never saw a disco done by tape before" advises Gerry (Smiles)

"Oh, it works for me" quips Dave (Laughs)

"Well, I like it" replies Gerry (Looks impressed)

Enter Terri ...

"Well, have you decided on an event?" asks Terri (Smiling)

"Yes, I have ... it's called CLIFF RICHARD - A CELEBRATION DISCO" replies Gerry (Smiles)

"What are we celebrating, Gerry?" asks Dave (Looks intrigued)

"I thought I would play old stuff first part followed by more up to date stuff in the second part" explains Gerry

"I like it" replies Dave (Smiles)

"Me too, Gezza ... Cliff's always been a favourite" replies Terri (Smiling)

"What happened after that?" asks Richard

"It just all snowballed from there" advises Gerry

"I had five years of very happy times and happy memories with all those people" explains Gerry

"Where are they now?" asks Richard (Looks puzzled)

"I really don't know what happened to any of them" adds Gerry

"But I've got another idea, Rich" replies Gerry

"What is it?" asks Richard

"Simply ... THE EVENT 2025 – DISCOTHEQUE" explains Gerry (Looks excited)

"Do you think you could bring all those people back together again?" adds Richard

"I'll try ... and I will ask them all to come to the event" replies Gerry

"Well, it sounds good" advises Richard

"By that time ... I will have come full circle" explains Gerry

THE EVENT 2025 ... REUNION

Everything starts to come together ... Richard and Gerry throw a party in Leeds, and the good times are back again!

Richard and Gerry meet again at the Crowne Plaza Hotel in Leeds ...

"So, what have you decided to do?" asks Richard (Sounds serious)

"I've decided to throw a reunion party here in Leeds" advises Gerry (Sounds excited)

"Where?" adds Richard (Looks intrigued)

"I thought of having it here at the Crowne Plaza Hotel" replies Gerry

"Who can you invite?" asks Richard

"We, mate ... you and I are throwing the party" explains Gerry

"I wouldn't know what to do" replies Richard (Sounds stunned)

"Don't worry about it I will see to that, Rich" advises

Gerry (Looks reassuring)

"Remember, I had five years of giving parties" explains Gerry

"I know how to put on a good show" adds Gerry

"We'll be the oldest swingers in town" laughs Richard

"Who cares?" laughs Gerry

"One more time, and it will be the coming together of everything" adds Gerry

"Who will we ask?" replies Richard (Sounds concerned)

"Everyone we can" advises Gerry (Smiling)

"Yea, but who exactly?" asks Richard

"Ex college friends ... ex Zodiac and Mirage's friends, all my friends at the Leeds General Infirmary ... I owe it to them" explains Gerry

"Besides we will have guests of honour attending too" adds Gerry

"Who are they?" asks Richard (Sounds intrigued)

"You and me ... we are the guests of honour, Rich" explains Gerry

"We'll do our own music ... it'll be the making of us both" adds Gerry

"Where will we stage it?" asks Richard

"I'm looking into that ... and I'll let you know soon" advises Gerry

EVERLASTING LOVE

"OK" replies Richard

Richard leaves the table and heads towards the Bar ...

Meanwhile, Gerry decides to talk to the Manager of the Crowne Plaza Hotel explaining the why's and wherefores of the upcoming event!

The Manager is up for it!

"Hi ... I'm Gerry" advises Gerry (Shakes hands with Manager)

"Hi ... I'm Alan ... nice to meet you" greets the Hotel Manager (Smiling)

Gerry explains his plan to Alan and asks for his opinion ...

"Well, Alan ... what do you think of my event?" asks Gerry (Smiles)

"Well, you can hold it right here in one of our suites" explains Alan

"We'll let you have it plus Bar facilities for £50" adds Alan (Smiles)

"It sounds like a bargain" replies Gerry (Smiling)

"How many can we invite?" adds Gerry

"Up to 100 ... is that OK?" asks Alan

"We do have a larger suite for up to 200" advises Alan

"Oh, I could have filled the 200 one many times over with my events for Zodiac back then" recalls Gerry

"What's stopping you now?" asks Alan (Sounds curious)

"Nothing really ... this is the event to end all events" explains Gerry

"Never say never" replies Alan (Smiling)

Richard returns to the table with a couple of drinks ... Gerry introduces Richard to Alan ...

"Rich, what do you think?" asks Gerry (Looks concerned)

"I think it's a good idea, but maybe a tall order to get people here" replies Richard

"Oh, don't worry ... I'll see what I can do" adds Gerry

Several telephone calls are made by Gerry in hope of inviting as many people as possible to the forthcoming event at the Crowne Plaza Hotel.

Gerry makes a Skype call on his laptop to Richard ...

"Well, how have you got on?" asks Richard

"I've asked ex colleagues I worked with, and found some Zodiac and Mirage members to come to our party" explains Gerry

"I've also invited staff from Leeds General Infirmary and some old college friends ... we should be OK" adds Gerry (Sounds cautious)

"Are they all up for it?" asks Richard (Sounds stunned)

"Yea, especially as I told them it was a reunion" explains Gerry

"We've got up to a 100 coming, Rich" adds Gerry (Smiles)

The scene is set for the upcoming Event reunion party ...

Gerry contacts Alan at the Crowne Plaza Hotel and gives him the good news!

"That sounds perfect ... what about music?" asks Alan

"Oh... I will take care of that, Alan" advises Gerry

"Can you help out with any disco equipment?" asks Gerry

"We've got double cd decks and lighting you can use" adds Alan

"Perfect, just perfect" replies Gerry (Sounds excited)

Alan invites Gerry to come into the Crown Plaza to view the facilities available for the event ...

Gerry shows Alan his Event File from his Zodiac days ...

"I'm really impressed, Gerry" advises Alan (Looks enthusiastic)

"Maybe we can work something out between us, as for something for the future" adds Alan (Smiles)

"Maybe" replies Gerry (Smiling)

"Did you hear that, Rich?" asks Gerry (Looks excited)

It's the night of THE EVENT 2025 REUNION PARTY ...

The music is scripted and ready to go ...

Richard and Gerry arrive in plenty of time at the Crowne Plaza Hotel in Leeds ...

Both are met by Alan, the General Manager ...

"A lot of guests have already arrived" advises Alan (Looks happy)

"Is everything ready, Alan?" asks Gerry (Looks serious)

"Yes ... it looks like you will have a good evening, Gerry" adds Alan

Gerry and Richard enter a packed suite ... and are greeted by everyone!

"Thanks for inviting us" advises an old college friend

"It's our pleasure" replies Gerry (Smiles)

"We're all going to have a good night tonight" adds Richard

"OK, I have to get to the music and start proceedings" adds Gerry

Richard continues to meet and greet everyone ...

Gerry prepares the music and opens the event ...

"Hi and welcome ... it's great to see you all here tonight" advises Gerry (Smiling)

"We're having a bit of a warm up now" explains Gerry

"The Event commences at 8pm ... but if you want to take to the dance floor now that will be fine" adds Gerry

"We'll have half an hour disco followed by half an hour slow music to get us in the mood" advises Gerry

The twin cd decks, and the lighting are quite

sophisticated ...

Gerry starts up the rehearsal ...

After thirty minutes of well-known disco anthems, Gerry changes the mood of the evening ...

"OK, we'll slow it down now for the next half hour" announces Gerry

"We'll put the music on auto pilot for the remaining half hour" explains Gerry

Richard and Gerry start to mingle with the guests ...

"Hi, Gerry and Richard ... lovely to see you again" greets a voice

"You, too" replies Gerry (Smiling)

"Who was that?" asks Richard (Looks intrigued)

"That was one of your old girlfriends, Lorraine ... do you remember her?" asks Gerry

"Oh, yea ... she was also at college, I remember" replies Richard

"You see ... you can remember some things" adds Gerry

"Lorraine was never my girlfriend, though" sighs Richard

"She was an old flame" laughs Richard

"Hey, look who's here" replies Gerry

"Who?" asks Richard (Looks around)

"Me old mate, Dennis from Mirage" adds Gerry (Looks

stunned)

"Good to see you Dennis, how are you?" asks Gerry

"How long has it been?" asks Dennis

"Over thirty years since we did Telethon mate" quips Gerry

"Do you remember that?" asks Gerry (Laughs)

"Yes, great days ... great days" laughs Dennis

"I miss the old days" adds Dennis

"I know we had good times there and at Zodiac" replies Gerry

It's now fast approaching 8pm, Gerry heads back to the DJ area to get things moving ...

An opening anthem opens the evening ...

"Hi, good evening and welcome to the Event 2025 reunion party" advises Gerry (Lots of clapping and cheering)

"It's a long time since I said that or put on a do" quips Gerry

"My mate, Rich, asked me tonight who were the guests of honour" adds Gerry

"Well, who are they?" asks Richard (Looks serious)

"You and me, mate ... we're the guests of honour" advises Gerry (Lots of clapping and shouting)

"We're celebrating all things disco here at the Crowne Plaza Hotel" adds Gerry

"Let the show begin" explains Gerry (Smiling)

"Are you all ready to party?" asks Gerry

Several hit recordings are now being played ...

The dance floor is almost full!

Alan, the General Manager wanders over to talk to Gerry at the DJ booth ...

"See, I told you it would be full, Rich" advises Gerry

"What about a regular slot here at the Crowne Plaza?" asks Alan

"What do you think, Rich?" asks Gerry

"We'll think about it" replies Richard

"OK ... let me know" advises Alan

"I will, Alan ... I will" replies Gerry

"Thank you again for a wonderful night" replies Alan

"I'm so glad everything is going so well" adds Alan

Richard and Gerry mingle with all their guests ... and to think it is now well over 50 years since they ventured into the HOLE IN THE WALL and the MECCA LOCARNO on Manningham Lane in Bradford!

Memories are really made of this!

EVERLASTING LOVE

DANCEHALL DAYS

DISCOTHEQUE NIGHTS

COPYRIGHT @2024
GERRY CULLEN

EVERLASTING LOVE

THE VATICAN MONSIGNOR

THE SAVIOUR'S COMING

*****5 STAR RATING ON AMAZON*

I thoroughly enjoyed The Vatican Monsignor by Gerry Cullen.

The character of Monsignor Kevin O'Flaherty is unique and intriguing, and I found myself rooting for him throughout his investigations.

The mix of mystical phenomena and religious undertones added depth to the storyline and kept me engaged from beginning to end.

The collaboration between Monsignor O'Flaherty and Professor Brookstein added an interesting dynamic to the plot, and I was hooked on the suspense and mystery that unfolded as they worked together to solve unknown phenomena.

Gerry Cullen's writing style is

captivating and kept me on the edge of my seat, making it difficult to put the book down.

Overall, I highly recommend The Vatican Monsignor to fans of mystery and intrigue, as it is a well-written and an engaging read.

LAURA (THE BOOKISH HERMIT)

***** 5 STAR RATING ON AMAZON

SKY HIGH!

COTE D'AZUR

"Sky High" by Gerry Cullen is an engaging thriller set against the breathtaking backdrop of the French Riviera. The story follows a Specialist Task Force composed of three 'ghost' operatives—Simon King, Steve McBride, and newcomer Bethany Williams—recruited to investigate the mysterious disappearance

of a British MI6 agent. With Countess Suzanna Minori at the helm, the group navigates both glamorous locales and complex crimes, blending action with a touch of intrigue.

Gerry's vivid descriptions of iconic destinations like Monaco, Monte Carlo, Nice and Cannes amplify the narrative's allure.

Overall, it's a captivating read that combines espionage with the charm of the Mediterranean coast.

- 4 STAR RATING ON AMAZON

LAURA (THE BOOKISH HERMIT)

EVERLASTING LOVE

DANCEHALL DAYS

DISCOTHEQUE NIGHTS

EVERLASTING LOVE

THE HOLE IN THE WALL

LOVE, MUSIC AND DANCING

DISCOTHEQUE

THE EVENT 2025 ... REUNION

COPYRIGHT - GERRY CULLEN 2024

MY NEXT PRESENTATION

THE VATICAN MONSIGNOR

ASH WEDNESDAY

GERRY CULLEN

Monsignor Kevin O'Flaherty is no ordinary priest. He loves the classics, has a taste for golf and Guinness, all things Irish, and has a nose for solving the unknown.

The Monsignor is Head of Investigations at the Vatican. He reports directly to Cardinal Raphael and His Holiness, the Pope ... Supreme Pontiff of Rome.

In this series of stories, The Monsignor, investigates

into various mystical phenomena, around the World.

The Monsignor is assigned by Cardinal Raphael and the Holy Father.
He teams up with Professor "Max" Brookstein in New York after being summoned by the Cardinal to check into recent ongoing unknown phenomenon.

In this latest series of stories, the Monsignor and Max investigate into codes and theories concerning The Turin Shroud, end of the World events and the Coronavirus pandemic.

PUBLICATION DATE

MARCH 2025

COPYRIGHT

GERRY CULLEN 2025

IF YOU ENJOYED READING ...

EVERLASTING LOVE

DANCE HALL DAYS

DISCOTHEQUE NIGHTS

IT'S A KIND OF LOVE ...

NOW AVAILABLE IN KINDLE/ PAPERBACK ON AMAZON

BASED ON AN ORIGINAL AND TRUE STORY

COPYRIGHT - GERRY CULLEN 2024

BETWEEN WORLDS:

MY TRUE COMA STORY

Gerry Cullen

GERRY CULLEN has written a unique and mesmerising book.

Gerry's true-life story includes an account of when he woke up after having major open-heart surgery in a Leeds hospital in March 2018. He received an unexpected gift from his induced coma.

Where had this gift of writing come from?
Why had he received it?

On reflection, Gerry now feels that he is incredibly lucky to have received this Heaven-Sent gift.
This life changing event and its aftermath have become a blessing in his life.

Gerry began to write profusely since that time; an astonishing development, as he had never authored any books or scripts before the coma.
Four years prior to his heart surgery, Gerry

experienced a spiritual awakening, and regular messages were coming to him in his dreams.
They were a major source of comfort to him.

Gerry believes that people in comas are living 'between worlds' and that their friends and family members are also living between worlds with them.

The messages from above have continued ever since and today his writing is flourishing. He has a fascinating tale to tell; it is a story of our times with many lessons for those with eyes to see and ears to hear!

The plot is a true-life account based around a fascinating subject of otherworldly connections.

Gerry's life story is full of encounters with another realm, the spiritual one.
The pacing is good throughout.
The book is well thought out as each chapter flows logically.

Author's Voice - The author's voice broadly means the written style of the book, covering tone, syntax, and grammar, amongst other things. It can be thought of as how the book is written.

Gerry is a good writer; I liked his style and voice. I was interested as the book progressed to discover more and it intrigued me.

This book could be a powerful memoir of Gerry's life and times, and the Heaven-Sent gift of writing that he received after open heart surgery.

I liked reading about his visions and encounters with the spirit world and the supernatural realm of life; it's quite fascinating.

I liked the examination of current events and times at the end of the book. too.

All in all, a great read for any person interested in life beyond our earth plane.

Many books have been adapted to film from this genre, for example, 90 Minutes in Heaven, an extremely popular movie, with over 1,800 reviews on Amazon Prime.

I feel that Gerry's book would make a great movie too.

It's a heart-warming and touching story of a man's journey and how he goes through a life changing operation that leaves him with a wonderful gift.

I loved the insights beyond our normal senses' range into another realm that will guide us if only we would allow it to do so.

In these times that we find ourselves in, I feel Gerry's testimony in the book, and his many anecdotes and stories, will demonstrate that there are more dimensions to behold than what we know in a three-dimensional world.

Report provided by Janet Lee Chapman, in September 2021, on behalf of Susan Mears Film and Literary Agency and Merlin Agency

ABOUT THE AUTHOR

Gerry Cullen

My first book, BETWEEN WORLDS: MY TRUE COMA STORY, is a true adaptation of what happened to me, before and after, having major open heart surgery at Leeds General Infirmary in March 2018.

It is a very real and true account of the "gift" I received after being in an induced coma.

All of my books, SKY HIGH! COTE D'AZUR, ANGEL'S EYES/CHRISTMAS ANGELS, THE VATICAN MONSIGNOR, IT'S A KIND OF LOVE and DCS MACCORMAC OXFORD and EVERLASTING LOVE are adapted from my series of stories, written for television.

I had never written books or for television prior to being in a coma.

My very real and true story continues today!

FOLLOW MY STORY ON TWITTER - @GerryCullen15

PRAISE FOR AUTHOR

Praise For Author Praise For Author Reviewed in the United Kingdom on 16 May 2022
An excellent book showing that there is far more to life then we realise and that there is a continuation of our soul after the death of our body.

Reviewed in the United Kingdom on 21 April 2022
Verified Purchase
With truly moving frankness the author narrates a life-threatening experience and how it brought him closer to his spiritual life.

Reviewed in the United Kingdom on 20 May 2022
A great read and one that really makes you think

Reviewed in the United Kingdom on 12 August 2022
This book was of particular interest to me because of my line of work. I love hearing about people's experiences with things that are on a different vibration to us earthly beings. The spiritual awakenings that people go through have been documented and discussed since the beginning

of time and each person's story is unique in its own way, there are always some similarities on the surface but I encourage you to look a little deeper - you can start with this book…….

The author begins by telling us a little about himself and his life growing up. He then goes into detail about the 'messages' he has received in dreams, these are set out in a sort of diary entry format. He also speaks of visions.

All of the incidents described seem quite insignificant on their own, but when you put them all together they give a much bigger and clearer picture.

There is a lot I could say about this book but seriously, we would be here all day! It's a great read that is sure to inspire and provoke discussion. It really doesn't matter what walk of life you are from, whether you are religious or a non believer. I feel the story should be taken for what it is and that is one gentleman's extraordinary, unique and beautiful experiences which he has chosen to share with the world.

The book, its content and the author himself are a true gift to the world.

5 stars

☐☐☐☐☐ - BETWEEN WORLDS: MY TRUE COMA STORY A 3 star rating on Amazon to date with no comments - SKY HIGH: COTE D'AZUR Reviewed in the United Kingdom on

13 December 2023

"Angels Eyes" by Gerry Cullen is a heartwarming and enchanting collection of seasonal stories that follows the adventures of Rebecca, Mary, John Paul, and Nicola, who have been reassigned by Michael the Archangel to become proprietors of the CHRISTMAS ANGELS shop in York. As they assume their roles as shopkeepers with a difference, the Angels become involved in a series of angelic and human situations that are filled with the magic of Christmas.

Set in various locations in York, the stories are imbued with a magical Christmas feeling that is sure to warm the hearts of readers. The characters' true identities as Angels are kept secret throughout the stories, adding an element of mystery and intrigue.

"Angels Eyes" is a delightful and uplifting read that captures the spirit of Christmas and the joy of the holiday season. Gerry Cullen's writing is engaging and filled with charm, making this book a perfect choice for anyone looking for a heartwarming holiday read. - ANGEL'S EYES: CHRISTMAS ANGELS No comments have yet been left for this book.
- THE VATICAN MONSIGNOR - THE SAVIOUR'S COMING

BOOKS BY THIS AUTHOR

Between Worlds: My True Coma Story

This true-life story includes an account of what happened to Gerry Cullen before and after waking up, having had major open-heart surgery at Leeds General Infirmary in March 2018, and the "gift" received from being in an induced coma. Gerry explains his new found gift within the book. But where it had come from and why he received it remains a mystery to this day.

Sky High! Cote D'azur

Nice, sun kissed jewel of the French Riviera. A popular tourist destination for the rich and famous.

When a British MI6 agent goes missing after being on attachment to the Commissariat de Police in Nice, a Specialist Task Force is set up on the Cote D'Azur to assist the Police in cracking crime on the Continent.

Three "Ghost Operatives" are drafted in by British Intelligence under an alias. Countess Suzanna Minori is placed in charge of unit in liaison with Mark Taylor in London.

In a series of assignments on the Cote D'Azur and in London suave Simon King, rough diamond Steve McBride and new recruit Bethany Williams are the "ghost" agents working under the code name: SKY HIGH!

Amazing picturesque locations on the French Riviera taking in Monte Carlo, Monaco, Cannes and Nice add to the charm, character and atmosphere of the series of stories.

Stylish, chic, gripping with just the right amount of panache!

Action adventure guaranteed!

C'est la vie!

Angel's Eyes/Christmas Angels

The Angel private eyes, with a difference, undertake anything with a twist, they are all real angels! Angel's: Rebecca, Mary, John Paul and Nicola have been sent by Michael the Archangel to LEEDS, West Yorkshire, and the ancient city of YORK to investigate all types of problems, from all levels of society. The Angel's are aiming to find, and guide, lost souls, to protect those in distress, and to help those without a cause. They have been charged to give sight to those who cannot see, whatever the problem, and to heal the sick and incurable. All the Angel's will have to undertake their assignments while also being human on Earth at the same time! They do not want to get their wings, they already have them! While under the protection of Heaven, they will also be able to cloak themselves in disguise!The Angel's are ready to assist anyone who needs their help in this stylish set of stories. The Angel's will encounter the Grey Lady, the ghostly Centurion and a cohort of Roman soldiers, Dick Turpin and Guy Fawkes along the way. The Angel's will also experience Speed Dating and various other problems in a very modern day World!

CHRISTMAS ANGELS - This seasonal set of stories reunites Rebecca, Mary, John Paul and Nicola. The Angel's have been reassigned by Michael the Archangel and assume the roles of Proprietors of the famous CHRISTMAS ANGELS shop in YORK, on a short term lease, with a view to being permanent! However, they are shop keepers with a difference! The Angel's become engaged in various angelic and human situations, all with a magical Christmas feeling! The stories take place at various settings in YORK. Will the Angel's be found out, or will their true identities remain an angelic secret?

It's A Kind Of Love

It's back to 1987 for this Singled Out themed comedy/drama series of stories set in Leeds.This book is based on an original, and true story, up to the end of 1991. What happens after that continues into 1992 with the ITV Telethon. Everything is based on real people, real parties and real events. The locations and venues of IT'S A KIND OF LOVE tell one man's story, and the challenges he faces, after joining a national Singles Organisation!

We commence in Leeds city centre, where various characters are introduced at Zodiac, and then again at Mirage.

Zodiac and Mirage are Social/Single Organisations which have been set up UK wide. Both are run privately, by the members.

This is a time when there were no mobile phones, laptops or the Internet! When we spoke of a tablet it was usually to take away pain, and not an electrical device connected to the Internet! Everyone used ordinary house telephones, and call boxes to get in touch, with each other. We used A to Z map books to find addresses and locations. Satellite for cars had not yet been invented!Pop music and fashions were top of the list.

Gez moves in to an apartment on the outskirts of Leeds, and decides to join Zodiac.

IT'S A KIND OF LOVE tells his real story!

From joining to attending parties, and events ... to meeting lots of ladies ... getting sound advice ... to running his own event disco's on a grand scale!

This all eventually leads to events for ITV TELETHON 1990 and 1992, and a main arena event in the grounds of HAREWOOD HOUSE on the outskirts of Leeds. But Gez is hiding something ...

Who is he, and where did he come from?

Why is he hiding a secret?

New adventures lie before him, but will he find love or won't he?

Why does he have so many female admirers at Zodiac?
Will all eventually be revealed?

Dcs Maccormac Oxford - Sanctum Sanctorum

Detective Chief Inspector Daniel MacCormac, now Chief Superintendent of Thames Valley Police, reports directly to the Chief Constable.

Sergeant Paddy Sheridan is now an Inspector based in Oxford, and still an endorsement of his old mentor, the Chief Super!

The dreaming spires of Oxford are the perfect backdrop to this series of stories.
A sartorial splendour of everything quintessentially English!

Oxford boasts fine University buildings clustered between other beautifully refined compact colleges and ecclesiastical structures. Oxford is also well known for it's elegance ... the Radcliffe Camera and the Bodleian library to mention just two of them.

Oxford is definitely one of England's most beautiful cities.

When the sudden retirement of Chief Superintendent Alex Samson takes place in Oxford, Detective Chief

Inspector Daniel MacCormac, is asked to take on the mantle of Chief Superintendent, by the Chief Constable of Thames Valley, Ben Gardiner.

MacCormac is reunited with his loyal colleague, Paddy Sheridan, who is successful in his own right, and is now an Inspector in Oxford.

Both undertake several investigations to find the truth, along with Pathologist, Mike Mortimer who assists them.

MacCormac and Sheridan investigate into sharp malpractice, ancient Egyptian codes and puzzles, Atropa Belladonna, Greek Mythology, Parasympathetic Rebound and a situation linking the Chief Superintendent to a murder at the Opera in Oxford!

The new Chief Superintendent will have to be at his best to outwit the those involved in all the investigations to bring them to justice!

The Vatican Monsignor: The Saviour's Coming

Monsignor Kevin O'Flaherty is no ordinary priest. He loves the classics, has a taste for golf and Guinness, all things Irish, and a nose for solving the unknown. The Monsignor is Head of Investigations at the Vatican. He reports directly to Cardinal Raphael and His Holiness, the Pope ... Supreme Pontiff of Rome.

In this series of stories, The Monsignor, investigates into various mystical phenomena, around the World.

The Saviour's Coming is based on the Blessed Trinity ... God in three persons, and it's the Monsignor's first investigation.

The Monsignor is assigned by Cardinal Raphael and the Holy Father. He teams up with Professor "Max" Brookstein in New York after being summoned by the Cardinal to investigate into recent, ongoing, unknown, unexplained phenomenon.

World governments are in a panic when earthquakes, famines and great signs appear in the sky ...

When an earthquake takes place in New York city, followed by the threat of a huge tidal wave, the Monsignor and "Max" devise a plan ... but will it work, and just how long do they have before it's too late? Is The Second Coming about to happen ... and does it signal the end of the World ... as we know it?

The Monsignor also investigates into ... The Ten Plagues of Egypt ... a phenomenon surrounding Mary Magdalen, the Arc of the Covenant and the Book of Galileo.

A gripping series of pulsating psychological, intrigue and mystery, with heart pounding twists and turns every step of the way! With a breath taking setting in Rome and around the World.

The adventure is just beginning!

Printed in Great Britain
by Amazon

57284121R00175